RED ONION MOUNTAIN

ISBN (Print): 978-1-950464-52-4
ISBN (eBook): 978-1-950464-53-1

RED ONION MOUNTAIN

KYLE OWENS

CHAPTER ONE

MY DEFINING MOMENT – I THINK

My name is Price Mullins, and I'm in Mrs. Collins' fifth-grade class. Now, I realize that my being in the fifth grade doesn't mean a whole lot in terms of world experience, but today I think I may have had me one of them things they call life-defining moments. I'm not positive as of yet, but I'm leaning toward it pretty hard.

It all began at school when I was throwing acorns at an oak tree after I had finished my lunch. I must have picked me up a good two or three handfuls of them things to toss at that big ol' tree, and do you know that I didn't hit that stupid thing nary a time! I was getting so frustrated that I thought I was going to bust.

But I was determined to hit that tree before I died. Or at least until we had to go back inside the school house. So I reached down and scooped me up a few more acorns to throw when she came up behind me, Mrs. Collins, that is, and asked me if I was going to spend my whole life throwing acorns at that there tree.

I told her I was just doing it temporarily, you know, just to pass the time until something better came along. Finding a way to pass the time until something better came along is kind of what fifth-graders do most of the time. Either that or finding themselves looking at their best buddy and wondering how in the world they were going to get something off before they got home and their mommy seen 'em.

Mrs. Collins put her hands on her hips and said a body couldn't make money throwing acorns at a tree, or at anything else for that matter, and that I should put my energy usage to better things. Why, even as dumb as I am, I know you can't make no living throwing acorns at a tree.

That's when she began talking to me about not wasting the day and how precious a thing time was (scolding me apparently wasn't considered a waste of time in her book) and then she began asking me what I wanted to do with my life.

Why, she was throwing questions at me faster than I could ever throw a handful of acorns, that's for sure!

I told her that I hadn't given it much thought on what I wanted to do with my life (which of course was a lie - I once thought about being a pig farmer until I found out what a pen full of pigs smelled like on a hot summer day; no thank you, I'll take my chances with acorn throwing), but I soon realized that even if I hadn't given my future much thought, Mrs. Collins apparently *had* given considerable thought to the matter of my life's work, because she pretty much told me right then and there what I was going to be doing when I got up big. You know how fifth-grade teachers are.

She said since I wrote good stories in English class I ought to be a writer.

I was so shocked that I dropped my acorns.

"A writer?" I said to myself. This ain't good. This ain't good at all. I can't be a writer. Why, I don't like writing, math, or anything whatsoever that even looks like school work in the smallest way. So to say that I might be a writer one day is something that I find so depressing it makes it difficult for me to go on. Those stories I wrote in English class was just homework, that's all they was.

However, she told me to give it a try because I had a great talent and I shouldn't waste it. I told her that I didn't know of any stories that I could write, so she told me that I should keep a little journal and write things in it every now and then. I could write down a joke, write a poem, tell what I did during the day, you know - just write whatever.

Well, when she got through telling me her plan for my life's work, I began thinking about it, and when I went home, I began thinking about it again. I guess if you're reading this, you can tell what I decided.

But I promise you that there'll still be no math!

That night after supper, I told Mommy what the teacher told me. She seemed happy about it and went on and on about how important writers were.

I asked Mommy if she knew of any important writers, and she told me no. I guess the writing field hasn't really grabbed ahold of society just yet.

Mommy then wanted to know if I was going to write me nonfiction or fiction. I had no idea what she was talking about. She then told me that nonfiction was true stories, like in a newspaper article, and fiction was stories made up, like anything my Uncle Willie says.

I told her I hadn't decided that yet. That's when she told me about an aunt of hers who tried to be a writer but gave it up when she got married. I think she was the same aunt that won a tobacco-spitting contest at the fair on her honeymoon. I assume her husband was either proud of her unusual skill set or maybe having some serious second thoughts about what he had just done.

Anyway, Mommy gave me some old envelopes and scrap papers to write on that she had laying around the house, and I piled them up on a table in my bedroom and tried to press all the wrinkles out of 'em as best as I could with a flat rock I got down near the outhouse.

I then marked on the top of one of the sheets, *MAY 1941*. I'm going to write down all the things that happen to me here on Red Onion Mountain.

I don't know what will become of it, but I reckon I'll find out soon enough.

Now, I've been doing me some thinking, and I have to say that I've never really seen my mommy like this before. You know, impressed with me. She's just so busy and all. She is always working, trying to make money for my three older sissies and myself. She'll do anything for money. Cook, clean, sew - whatever needs to be done, she can sure do it. And she's great at it, too.

I don't have a daddy. Not long after I was born he killed himself with a shotgun.

CHAPTER
TWO

LOVE CIRCLES

Mary - that being my oldest sissy - has a boyfriend, and he comes over to our house just about every day since they got going good together. He's tall and skinny. To be honest, he looks like a pine tree without any limbs on it. We're all afraid to have him go out into the woods by himself in fear that someone might try and cut him down for firewood.

Now that Mary has a boyfriend, me and Suzie and Sally - them's my other two sissies - have been teasing her something fierce. I don't think Mary likes it too much, but we sure do.

The boy that she likes is named Junior. They met at the store that his daddy owns. Mommy always goes in there and trades every Saturday. Well, if she has enough money and if she doesn't she has to wait until the next Saturday.

I reckon when Mary and Junior saw into one another's eyes over a stacked pile of castor oil bottles that they decided right then and there they had to have each other. But just between you and me, I think meeting your boyfriend or girlfriend over a pile of castor oil bottles should be considered a dire warning. But of course that's just me thinking on this here paper.

Funny thing about Junior is that I don't know what his real name is. I know he's a Junior, but I don't know what he's a Junior of. The store owner is called Wart, but I don't think that's his real name unless, of course, he was raised by frogs or a witch. And I know that Mommy wouldn't allow Mary to hitch up with a family that had a witch in it. I would be mighty curious about the frog family idea, though.

It's kind of odd that my not knowing his real name just occurred to me. I guess writing does help you think. Well, if you can call this thinking.

Anyway, I seen Mary and Junior holding hands yesterday as they walked around the house. Seems like that's all they really do. Why, they've already worn a path all the way down to the dirt. They don't really talk much when they walk, either. Unless of course they're yelling at me to stop throwing rocks at them. Otherwise they just kind of giggle and smile. They probably get so dizzy walking in circles that they can't think of anything to say.

Mommy told me and Suzie and Sally to stop teasing Mary and her boyfriend. Mommy said one day we'd fall in love and we wouldn't like a bunch of kids making fun of us. That's probably true, but if I do fall in love, I hope we do more than just walk in circles like some sort of crazed cow.

CHAPTER
THREE

GONE FISHING

Me and Sally went fishing today. School is out for the summer, so I can spend all my time fishing and such. Sally is a pretty good fisher. She is two years older than me, but we seem to get along the best.

We fish the Pound River, which ain't too far from the house. We have this spot we always go to at the water's edge on this big ol' boulder. It's flat on top so we don't have to worry about our can of worms rolling into the river. The river's not very deep, although it has gotten that way after a few good-sized rains.

I'd say we fished for about twenty minutes when Sally got a bite. She started reeling it in and, boy, did she start giving me the business about how she had got the first fish of the day and that by doing so she was bringing glory to womanhood all over the world.

Well, when she reeled her catch in a little farther, she started screaming like a mule that backed into a barbed fence.

She had up and caught herself the biggest water snake that I had ever seen in my life. It had to be five feet long! When she realized what she had caught she threw her pole just about as far as she could and then headed up into the woods, womanhood and all, and hid behind a tree.

I didn't exactly know what I was supposed to do. That snake just laid on that rock turning in every direction that it could think up to try and get loose from that hook. Sally began yelling at me, "Throw the pole into the water and be done with it!" But I decided against that. A man doesn't throw a perfectly good fishing pole away like that. Why, I'd more likely throw Sally into the river than that there pole. A fishing pole is a tool which you can use again and again, which makes it very valuable to a boy like myself. Sally's just my sister.

So I went over to that snake and prayed me a quick prayer and really took stock of the situation. That's when I took my foot and placed it on top of that snake's head and then reached down and grabbed ahold of it behind the head with my right hand and looked at it pretty hard.

Sally started screaming, "What in the world are you doing? Put that snake down and get up here in these woods right now or I'm telling Mommy on you!"

I thought that was being a little bit dramatic, but I also understood her position. Not many sissies want to see their brother bit by a snake on a big boulder.

But as it turns out, when you hold a snake in your hand, you are pretty much committed to the situation. Now, I was a little bit too scared to pull the hook out because I didn't want to get bit and die. So I just took my knife and cut the line and decided that I was going to just throw the snake back into the river hook and all.

The terrible thing is, here I was holding a snake in my hands and all I could think about was when I go to throw him into the river, he's going to turn around and bite me.

But a boy can only hold a snake for so long before he comes to the conclusion that he needs to get rid of the thing.

So I took a deep breath and counted to three (okay, I'll admit that I counted to three more than one time), and then tossed that snake back into the water with the hook still in its mouth.

At least that's what I tried to do.

What happened was that it had wrapped its tail around my wrist and wouldn't let go, even when I tried to throw it. So here I was with a snake dangling from my wrist, twisting and turning in every direction, with my only wish being for it to let me go, and its apparent only wish was not wanting to let go.

I have to admit that I did scream at this point. I don't remember what I said or even if it was actually a true word of any kind, but scream I did.

Then the snake fell onto the rock, and I jumped back and fell backward off the rock and onto the bank.

That's when I remember yelling "It's going to kill me!" Them words I remember quite clear.

Thankfully, it didn't kill me. When I stood back up, and I did so pretty quickly, I seen that it wasn't on the rock anymore. It had apparently got off the rock and fell back into the water, because I seen something swimming away.

Sally came over and asked, "Is it gone?"

"Yeah, it's gone," I said and we both took turns fishing with my pole since hers didn't have a hook on it anymore.

I thought I had been pretty brave during the whole situation, but my sissy thought I was just plain stupid for grabbing hold of a snake that could kill me.

I have to admit that her observation was not without merit.

When the day was done, we had caught us one trout and three bluegills. Oh, and one snake.

CHAPTER
FOUR

THIS IS BILLY

Well, love has struck the Mullins household yet again.

Billy, my friend from down the road about a mile, came over to show me his new coon dog. While showing it off, he caught eye of Suzie, and I could practically hear the thud of his fast-beating heart.

I asked after the dog's name, but Billy was way too busy watching Suzie through the living room window while she was doing her sewing to hear anything I was asking him about. Why, I think I could have been on fire right there beside him and he wouldn't even have noticed.

My sissies don't go to school because they help mommy with her sewing business or anything else she might be doing, so Billy doesn't get to see them there. Not much at home either, as we don't usually play at my house. But something about that day made him really notice her for the first time - he wouldn't take his eyes off of her.

He then started heaving questions at me about what she was like and what her favorite color was.

"What in the world do you want to know that for?" I asked.

He said, "I need all the background information I can get so I can use it to help win her over."

I told him that I had no idea what her favorite color was. Then I asked him what his favorite color was and he reckoned it was blue. So I told him that we would just go with that then.

Next he wanted to know if Suzie had her a boyfriend. I got to thinking that was probably the first piece of background information he needed, but I told him that she didn't have no boyfriend, and that seemed to please him pretty good.

Then I asked him again if his dog had a name. He said Percy. Then he wanted to know if Suzie might want to see Percy. I just shook my head and told him I'll see and went inside to get this dumb day over with.

As soon as I entered, Suzie asked who that ugly redheaded kid with the big ears was. Billy was going to be in an uphill battle for the hand of Suzie, I knew.

I told her it was Billy and he wanted to know if she wanted to see his new coon dog. I didn't mention marriage or anything like love, in hopes Billy might have some chance with her by springing his love on her in a more gradual way. And I reckon showing her his coon dog is just about the most gradual way a man can confess his love to a woman as can be.

Suzie went out and got down on her knees and started petting the dog. I noticed Billy wasn't looking so good. He was shifting his weight from leg to leg, and he was sweating like a pig out of season. Then his eyes went back into his head and he simply passed out right then and there and fell straight away onto the ground.

That boy was so in love that he had up and fainted! I had never heard or seen of that before. I tried to wake him up as Suzie looked on, a little scared. She asked me what happened to him, and I told her the truth - that I think he fainted. Then I asked her what her favorite color was. She looked at me like I was crazy.

"What's that got to do with anything?" she finally said.

I told her that Billy was wanting to know.

"I guess I like blue," she told me.

"I guess it has a chance of working out then."

That brought a confused look to Suzie's face.

"Price, what in the world are you talking about?" she yelled at me.

"He likes blue, too," I told her.

I don't think she ever did catch on to what I was saying. Then I told her to go get Mommy, but Suzie said she was gone to deliver a blanket she had made to the store. Then I told her to go get Mary, but she said she went with Mommy. That's when Sally came running outside, and I just knew that our little disaster here was about to get about five times bigger.

Sally looked down at Billy and asked, "Which one of you all shot him?"

"Nobody shot anyone, you dumb girl," I said.

Then she asked what happened, and I told her. She asked why he fainted, and I said because he was in love with Suzie. When Suzie heard that comment, she looked at me with her mouth wide open.

I think my "Billy likes blue" comment earlier was starting to make sense to her now.

Then Sally got down and laid right on top of Billy like he was her bed and put her nose right up against Billy's nose and said, "I think he's dead."

Well, that put Suzie in a panic, and she took off running inside screaming that her beauty had up and killed somebody and they was going to put her in jail.

I just shook my head and went to the well and got a bucket of water and brought it over and told Sally to move. I threw it right on poor ol' Billy's face. He woke up instantly, and I turned to Sally and told her, "I knew he wasn't dead."

Sally said that's good.

Then I told her to go tell Suzie. So she went inside and Billy just sat on the ground looking as if he had just been baptized for the Lord.

He asked me what happened, and I told him that he appeared to have passed out. He asked me if Suzie noticed. I told him it was kind of hard for her not to notice, being he did his passing out right there in front of her while she was petting his Percy. Then he laid back down on the ground and spread his arms and legs out and looked right at me and told me to kill him.

He said that he couldn't go on in this life knowing that Suzie had actually seen him faint. Well, I told him that I understood that he's embarrassed by passing out in front of a girl that he had just fallen in love with two minutes before, but I don't think me killing him was a well-thought-out idea. And I didn't have anything to kill him with anyhow.

But he said I could kill him with the bucket, but I argued that would take pert near all day and I'd rather be doing other things than beating him in the head with a bucket.

Poor ol' Billy got up and wrung out the water as best he could from his clothes and decided to head on back home. Even his coon dog looked a little depressed as they walked off.

But before he got gone, I caught up to him and told him Suzie told me that her favorite color was blue. This made a smile come to his face for a few seconds, then he headed on back home in a happier mood than he had started out with.

There is just no two ways about it, though: Love is the most humiliating thing a boy can go through.

CHAPTER FIVE

BATS

Sally and I decided that we'd go fishing again this morning. We're pretty much addicted to it, as Mommy says. I don't know why, but I like to fish better than anything else in this world. Sally, too.

As we got ready, Sally told me that Mary and Mommy came home yesterday evening by way of the train tracks behind our house, and Mary told her it was a whole lot closer to our fishing spot by going that way than by going down the road like we usually do. Well, I didn't care which way we went as long as we went. So down the railroad tracks we headed.

As we walked, we talked a little bit about Billy and Suzie, and Sally wanted to know if I thought they'd get married. I told her I didn't have the slightest idea, and Sally said she didn't think they would because Billy's ears were too big and that was a sign of a poor lover. In fact, she said it was the number one sign! I asked her what that had to do with anything and she said big ears used up too much blood flow. And if you use up all your blood flow on your ears there wouldn't be enough for the other thing.

I asked her what she meant by the other thing and she just giggled. I always get scared when one of my sissies giggles like that. It usually means love stuff or that someone put something in my shoes that wasn't supposed to be there. And I didn't feel anything peculiar in my shoes at that moment.

To be honest, I don't think Sally has enough blood flow to her brains.

We walked us a spell more when we came to a railroad bridge and I stopped and said we can't walk across that bridge because we'd meet a train for sure, and that would be quite a jump to the ground there or we'd end up falling into the small stream beneath it and get all muddy. And there's one thing Mommy don't like, and it's washing muddy clothes. We'd get switched for sure if we did that.

Sally agreed, so we decided in order to get across to the other side that we'd walk underneath the bridge, then hop along on some rocks sticking out of the stream so we wouldn't get our feet all wet. Then we'd walk up the other side of the hill and continue on our way. I reckon that was a pretty good plan.

I went under the bridge first and walked through the tiny stream to the bank on the other side and was about to walk up the hill when I heard Sally screaming.

I turned around and ran back down to her right quick. She was looking up into the underside of the bridge screaming and hollering like she had seen a ghost or something. Well, I got to looking and seen up in the underneath of that bridge the biggest bunch of upside down bats that I had ever seen in my life!

I'd like to of said I didn't yell, but it would be a lie.

I grabbed Sally by the arms, then put my hand over her mouth and whispered to her to stop her screaming or them bats would come down out of there and eat us.

Sally's eyes got big at that point. Though I'm not sure if it was because of what I said or if she couldn't breathe with my hand over her mouth.

I whispered to her, "I'm going to take my hand off of your mouth. Now, when I do, you can't scream. Do you understand what I'm saying?"

She nodded that she understood, and I took my hand off her mouth kind of slowly as I watched them bats to make sure they didn't try and dive bomb us right there.

Well, it wasn't even a second after I removed my hand when she started screaming again, and before I knew it, we both ran back home as fast as we could and told Mommy about what we saw. She said she didn't think they would hurt us any, but me and Sally decided when we go back fishing we would take the long way around.

Mary said if we got bitten by a bat we would probably turn into a vampire. I didn't exactly know what a vampire was until she told me it was someone that gets bitten and then they go around and bite people and suck all their blood. Mommy said that sounded more like a banker.

Sally started to cry and I started - well - I'll just say that I became real tense. I don't know if Mary knew of what she was saying or not, but I know that I will never ever go under that bridge again.

CHAPTER
SIX

VISITING BILLY

I spent the morning in my bedroom measuring the size of my ears. I don't know why, but I did. Well, I know why, but I don't want to say. I'm sure you can guess. They measured a little over an inch or so. I don't know what that means, but that's what the ruler said.

After I did my measuring, I went over to Billy's to see what he was up to. When I got there, Billy was on the front porch with a sack, and his dog Percy was playing in the yard. I went over to Billy and asked, "Why didn't you come over this morning?"

He just humped his shoulders and said, "I couldn't come over there after what happened the other day. I'd be too embarrassed."

I said to him, "What in the world would you be embarrassed for? I mean we've all done stuff that we wish we hadn't done. That's just life."

He just looked down at the ground and I decided to leave it at that.

"What are you going to do with the sack?" I asked.

"Mommy wants me to go up in the woods and get her some ramps. Do you want to help?"

I told him I would. It would give me something to do.

Now, for those that might not be in the know, ramps are kind of like a wild onion or a wild leek. And if you eat a couple of them raw, you are going to have some of the worst breath in these here mountains. It's kind of like garlic. It seems like the only reason to eat ramps is out of meanness, because no one can stand to be close to you after you eat a mess of 'em.

We headed up the hill to where he knew the ramps were, and he stopped and asked me straight out, "Would you object to me trying to date your sister?"

"Which one?"

He looked at me kind of funny and said, "I was assuming Suzie. Do you think I should date a different one?"

"Well, you can't date Mary because she has a beau. So your choice is either Suzie or Sally."

"I don't remember much about Sally. Is she pretty?"

I told him, "A brother can't judge the prettiness of his sissies. It's not normal."

"Do you think she would like me?" he asked with a hint of a grin on his face.

"I know that when you were lying on the ground all passed out, she laid right on top of you and put her nose up against your nose."

"Why did she do that for?"

"To see if you were dead."

"Is that how they do it now?"

"It's how Sally does it."

"I've never had a girl lay flat on top of me before. I wished I was awake when it happened."

"You didn't miss anything by being fainted. Plus, she said you was dead and no man wants a girlfriend that can be that wrong. And her saying that you was dead absolutely scared Suzie to death."

This comment got Billy all excited in the face. It was like someone had given him a big cake or something.

"Suzie was worried about me?" he asked, grinning from big ear to big ear.

"No. She was worried she would have to go to jail because her beauty had killed you."

"I would have testified that it wasn't her fault if I had died."

"You couldn't have testified if you was dead, Billy."

"Well, I could have wrote a letter or something."

I didn't even try to argue the point. I think he's so in love that he's not thinking straight.

After we got us our sack of ramps we headed back to his house. He took the ramps to his mommy in the kitchen. She was happy with them.

We headed into the living room and I seen his radio on a table up against the wall. I told him how lucky he was to have a radio because we didn't have one. He told me that his daddy likes to listen to Jack Benny. I didn't really know who he was, but I guess from the way Billy told it that he would tell a lot of jokes and so forth.

We never had a radio and probably never will. They just cost too much money for Mommy to even hope to buy one, let alone get one in real life. He sure is lucky to have a radio.

He's also lucky that he has a daddy.

CHAPTER SEVEN

NO MORE SCHOOL

I got up this morning and fixed me some toast for breakfast and got me a jar of water to wash it down with. For some reason I like my toast burnt. I don't know why, but I do. Mary said it was probably because I was missing some vitamins that made me crave it burnt, and Sally said it was because I was just dumb.

My sissies were still in bed, as usual. They always sleep late because they say they need their beauty sleep. But to be honest, I don't think either of them could sleep that long.

My mommy came into the kitchen and knelt down in front of me. She acted like something was on her mind, and I have to say that I was getting a little bit worried.

She told me that I couldn't go to school anymore because she didn't have the money to pay for it. She was crying, she found it so hard to tell me. I guess I kind of knew this would happen because Mary, Suzie, and Sally never completed school either. Mary got the furthest. She was in the seventh grade.

I guess things like this happen. Of course they seem to happen more to us than others.

Mommy then hugged me and told me that she felt like she had failed me. I told her not to think like that because she could never fail me. That would be impossible. She then went into the living room and sat down with her head in her hands.

I've never felt so sad in my life than when I saw my mommy like this. It's not her fault. In fact, I don't think it's anybody's fault. It's just the way it is.

Later on I got to thinking that it was kind of odd the way I felt about not being able to go to school anymore, because I didn't really like school, but now that I can't go, I feel different about it. If I don't go to school, I'd rather it be on my terms than on the fact that we can't pay for it.

But I think I will keep writing. I kind of enjoy it. I've noticed when I go to bed and I forget to write something down in my journal, I feel guilty and have to get up out of bed to write it down. I don't know what that means, but that's how I feel.

I'm on the front porch as I write this. Its night, so I have a candle burning here on the porch rail so I can see. I can hear the frogs in the swamp by the railroad track cutting a shine. Mary and Mommy are sewing a quilt for the Robinson family in the living room. I think the Robinsons are rich. It's kind of hard for me to tell who is rich and who is not, because everyone seems rich when compared to us.

Suzie is reading a book, I don't know of what. Sally, well, I don't know where she is. I guess she went to the outhouse. Mommy said that Sally goes to the outhouse so much that she was afraid she was turning into a middle-aged man.

Billy came over at around noon today and told me that he lost his new coon dog. He got up this morning and spent the day looking for it, but never could find it. He was hoping that it had come here, but I told him that I hadn't seen it.

Suzie said hi to Billy and he turned solid red. I guess he still hasn't overcome his embarrassment from his fainting spell. Sally then showed up and said hi to Billy, too, and then she started staring at his ears. I told her to stop looking at Billy's ears like that, and she said she'd do as she pleases.

Billy started to feel uncomfortable and decided he'd go on and look for his dog somewhere where there weren't any girls around. I told him I hoped he found Percy and he walked down the road rubbing his ears.

I guess I'll get ready for bed now. There's nothing else to do.

CHAPTER
EIGHT

SNAKE IN THE OUTHOUSE

Rattlesnake! Rattlesnake!

I'm still shaking over what just happened. I was going to the outhouse and I opened the door like I always do. I pulled down my pants and underwear and I sat down, and it just so happened I looked to my left, and there it was.

It was the biggest snake I have ever seen in my life! As soon as I looked at it, it started to rattle. I didn't have to think for even a second on what I should do because I just got up and charged on outta there with my pants around my ankles just as fast as I could. I actually think that I flew!

I barely got outside the door when I fell, but I wasn't going to waste any time trying to get up, so I just started rolling away from the outhouse like a big log rolling down a hill. I just knew that thing was behind me and was going to bite me any second!

I stopped rolling when I got several feet away from the outhouse. I just looked at the outhouse wondering what I should do. That's when I decided I best pull up my pants.

I slowly started walking back to the outhouse to see if that snake was still in there. I opened the door a crack and seen it still curled up in there beside the hole. It was probably still laughing at me and the sight of my little white hiney bolting out the door like a white sheet blowing in a tornado.

Everyone else was gone into town, so I was there by myself, but I knew I had to get rid of that there serpent. We didn't have a gun because Mommy won't allow one in the house after what Daddy did. So I went over to the shed and got the hoe. I went back to the outhouse and opened the door and looked in.

That snake was still there. I raised up the hoe with my left hand and sort of used my right hand to balance and then I slammed the hoe down onto that snake as hard as I could to cut it in half!

Well, that was the plan, anyway. What actually happened was all I did was knock the snake off onto the floor. So I turned and ran away a few steps. Of course, I guess running almost to the front porch of the house is a little more than a few steps, but I tell you what, I was scared.

I then walked back to the outhouse realizing I had to be a man about this. I can't run from it, I had to face it down and kill it.

I went around the side of the outhouse to see if I could see where the snake was. I thought it might have crawled out, but I didn't see it, so I figured it had to be still inside. So I opened the door using my hoe and looked all around. I didn't see it on the floor at first.

Then I heard it. It had managed to get up into the rafters in the ceiling, and its evil eyes were looking straight at me.

So I opened the outhouse door as wide as I could and lifted my hoe. I was going to hit that snake as hard as I could and cut his head clear off. I took me a big swing but only hit one of the rafters in the ceiling and then slammed my face into the handle of that hoe.

I thought I was gonna die, it hurt so bad! I turned and stumbled away from the outhouse, and I could hear that snake laughing. I never felt so stupid in all my life. I about killed myself with a hoe! Why, that's something even city people are too smart to do. I tell you what's the truth – if I had died at the hands of my hoe, everybody in town would have come to my funeral just to laugh.

My nose started to bleed a little, so I took out my handkerchief (Mommy says that all little boys need a handkerchief because they're little boys) and tended to it while I looked back into the outhouse. That's when I saw the snake crawling out the top of the outhouse. I ran around the back and saw it fall to the ground and slither away and disappear into some weeds.

It was gone, and I sure was happy about that.

When Mommy and my sissies came back I told 'em what happened. They're still laughing.

But I got that snake out, didn't I?

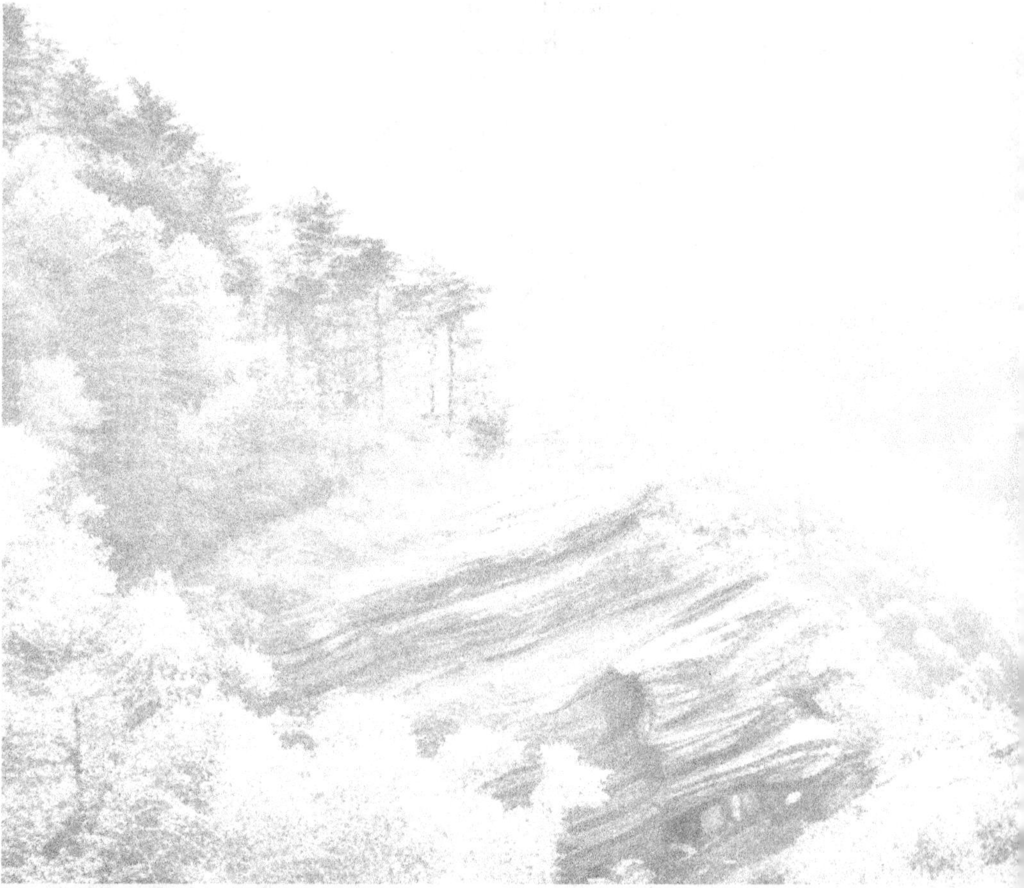

CHAPTER
NINE

BILLY AND THE BRIDGE

Billy and I went walking along the train tracks this morning because I told him about them bats that me and Sally had seen the other day, and he bugged me to death to take him to 'em so he could see 'em with his own eyes. I told him to go himself and then he said I was scared, which I was, too, but I wasn't going to admit to it, so I finally said I'd take him.

Of course, I did tell him that he was a fine one to be talking about being scared being that he fainted at the sight of Suzie. It got a little ugly after that as we double-dog dared each other. Him daring me to go to the bridge and me daring him to go talk to Suzie, but that's what friends are for, I reckon.

So we headed down the track so he could see how big them bats were. I told him they didn't look giant or anything like that, but they were still bats.

We got about halfway there when we seen an animal on the side of the track that had been run over by a train. It had been cut completely in half and was covered in flies and maggots. As we got closer to it we both realized that it was Billy's coon dog, Percy.

Billy looked like he was going to cry, and I probably wasn't too far from joining him, but we both was able to keep from balling. I picked up Percy's back half and Billy picked up his front half and we took him up into the woods and buried him by piling rocks on top of him. Billy asked me if I would say something over the grave, you know, like a preacher.

I didn't know what to say, but I did know what I couldn't do: I couldn't tell Billy no.

So I said, "Percy was a good dog. Even though God didn't let him live very long on this earth, we sure will miss him. He brought joy to Billy's life, and I was sure glad to have met him. I think dogs are very important to this world because if there was no dogs then we'd be left with cats, and you can't do anything with a cat - or sissies, for that matter."

That's when Billy told me that I was getting off topic, so I just said, "In Jesus' name, amen."

Then we both began howling like coon dogs as our version of a twenty-one gun salute.

I guess it's kind of dumb to go to so much trouble over a dead animal, but me and Billy thought it was important, and that's all that mattered.

We then went on down to the bridge, and the closer we got the more careful we was. We slowly went down the hill at the railroad bridge and looked up into the underneath side of it and there them bats were. There had to be hundreds of them.

Billy said that he had never seen so many bats in his life in one place, and I had to agree with that. Then Billy wanted to know how they could tell each other apart because they all looked the same, and I told him I reckon they got it all figured out because they weren't fighting any.

That's when I got to looking and seen on the ground a whole lot of bat poop laying around. It looked really deep and had a very strong smell. I'd sure hate to fall in that.

Well, as soon as I said that to myself, Billy being Billy slipped and fell right in the middle of all that poop. He started yelling and crying for me to get him out.

I reached out my hand and told him to be quiet or he'd wake up all them bats and we'd be vampires by nightfall and be eating blood for supper. He didn't give me no mind, though, because his screams got louder.

I grabbed his hand and pulled as hard as I could, but he was stuck like no one had ever been stuck before. It was like them bats had been pooping concrete, and Billy was going to be stuck in there forever. I told him I'd have to go get some help, but he begged me not to leave him, so I didn't.

He then finally stopped screaming, not because he was calming down but because his throat was starting to hurt.

He looked at me in all sincerity and said, "If I die here in all this bat poop, please tell everyone that I died some other way."

I asked him what he wanted me to tell everyone, and he said he didn't know, but it should be something heroic. Maybe saving a child on a railroad track. I told him that would be a good story, but people would want to meet the child for a grand ceremony to celebrate his bravery.

So he thought about it some more and said that I could tell everyone that he tried to save a cow from being run over by a train. I didn't really think that was very heroic, but it was a better story than dying in bat poop. So we shook on it.

But I'm happy to say that Billy didn't die in that smelly poop because I finally managed to pull him out. We got out from underneath the bridge and Billy stood there with his hands out to his side looking down at himself. Then he said that fainting in front of Suzie was no longer the worst day of his life.

He went down to the stream under the bridge and told me to watch in case somebody came. Then I heard him jump in, and I looked and saw him in a deep pool area with all of his clothes on. When he got situated in the water, he took his clothes off and tried cleaning them as best he could, and himself as well.

"My mom is going to skin me alive when I get home," he shouted. But I didn't think he had any worry about that because he stunk so bad that she wouldn't be able to stand getting close enough to him to switch him any.

Then being that I didn't really have anything to do, I picked up a rock and threw it in the water near him and shouted, "Gator!" which made him give out an awful scream and caused me to laugh pretty hard. I told him it wasn't a real gator, but the humor didn't really hit him at the moment.

That's when the unexpected happened. Out of nowhere I heard someone ask, "What are you laughing at?"

Well, I almost jumped out of my skin in fear! I had no idea anyone was around. It turned out to be Suzie, and it was at this exact moment that Billy came walking up the embankment naked as he could be.

He seen Suzie and Suzie seen him and I saw both of them doing their seeing. They both let out screams and took off a-running in opposite directions.

I watched Suzie disappear around the curve of the tracks and heard a large splash from where Billy had done and jumped back into the stream.

I have to say that I felt pretty terrible about the whole thing. I was supposed to be watching in case someone came, but I was too busy picking on Billy and didn't see Suzie coming up the tracks. Some friend I am, not to mention a bad brother for not saving Suzie from seeing all of Billy that there was to see.

I yelled down to Billy and told him that she was gone and he could come back out now. He yelled back that he didn't believe me.

I can't say as I blame him none. I would have felt the same way, but he did finally get out of the water. He let his clothes dry out with a good sunning.

He told me that he didn't know if he would ever speak to me again. I told him my side of the story, which in truth there wasn't one, and told him that I was in the wrong. He did seem to lighten up a little as we headed home. I asked him if there was something I could do to maybe make up for it somehow, and he said he'd have to think about it.

My guess is that's what Suzie is doing right now, thinking about it.

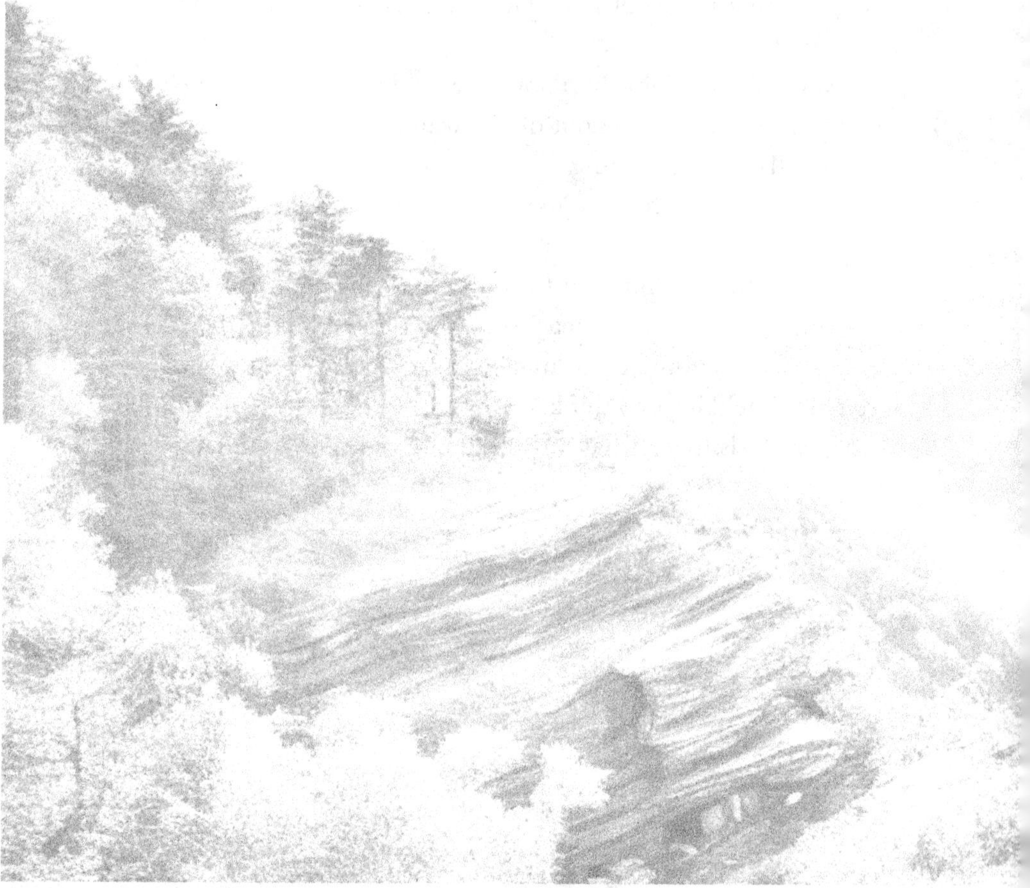

CHAPTER TEN

THE LETTER AND THE HAUNTED HOUSE

Mommy got a letter today from her brother who is in the Navy and is stationed somewhere far off. He seems to like it pretty good, and he's met some new friends, and Mommy was sure happy to hear from him.

He talked a lot about trying to prove himself, which got me to thinking about how *I* could prove myself. With Mommy having to do so much work to pay the bills, I've begun thinking that maybe I should do something to try and help instead of just fishing and such. Though fishing does put food on the table.

Mary looks more and more like she's going to marry off soon. Junior has a plan to go to Knoxville and try and find some work because there's nothing around here but coal mines, and he doesn't want anything to do with that.

I guess I can't blame him none, but a man has to do what he has to do to take care of his family. That's sort of the predicament I'm in right now, you know - thinking how I could help and all. Be a man. Prove myself like Uncle Peter. Maybe one day I'll join the Navy and meet up with him on the Arizona. That's the name of the ship he's stationed on. We'll see.

But what I didn't expect was how Uncle Peter's letter was going to inspire Billy. You see, they say the old Simmons house up in Hoot Owl Hollow is haunted. Now, I don't know if that's true or not, but me and Billy was walking to the store the other day and we stopped in front of it and wondered if the stories we heard about it was true.

I have to say that it sure looked haunted. It had vines and trees growing up all around it, and a few windows were broken out and the roof didn't look too safe either.

Billy said maybe we should go in there one night and see for ourselves if it's haunted or not. I asked him if he was crazy and he told me that I'd known him long enough now to know that he was.

Turns out that by me telling him about the letter from my uncle also got Billy thinking about how to prove himself, and he wanted to do something that no one else would do.

I told him if he goes into that house at night he will definitely be doing something that no one else would do for any amount of money in the world. We then went on to the store and I gave it no more thought until that evening.

It was nearly six o'clock when I looked out the window and seen Billy walking up the road. I ran outside to see what he was doing and seen that he was toting a flashlight and a big stick.

Now, I know anytime I see a man or boy carrying a flashlight and a stick that he's surely up to something. Either Billy was going to look for frogs or he was up to a kidnapping. And I knew that Billy wasn't the kidnapper type, so I asked if he was going to do him some frogging.

"Nope," he said. "I'm going to spend the night in that haunted house."

I stared at him like you do the two-headed cow at the fair. You just don't think what you're seeing is real. I told him, "You crazy thing, you can't go in there or them ghosts will get you for sure."

I asked him if his mommy knew what he was doing, and he said he told her that he was spending the night with me and that I needed to cover for him. He asked me if I'd do that for him and I told him I would.

I thought about going with him, but he said to prove himself he had to do it alone. So then I watched him walk on down the road toward that haunted house, and I just shook my head in wonder and hoped he really knew what he was getting himself into.

Well, I found out at about two in the morning what he got himself into when I heard him knocking on my bedroom window. The sound of that knocking really put a fright into me because I could see his shadow standing in the window because of the big moon and I was feared something fierce.

Before I fell asleep, I had been thinking about Billy in that haunted house all night and wondering how he was doing, so I had ghosts on top of ghosts running through my mind. So when I seen that shadow looking in on me, I was rightfully sure that something dead had up and crawled out of the ground and was now outside and about to figure out what I tasted like.

But then it called out my name and it sounded more like Billy than a ghost, so I went over to the window and opened it, and sure enough there was Billy shaking like a bucket of leaves inside a big ol' windstorm with his stick in one hand and his flashlight in the other.

I asked him if he was okay, but he didn't say anything. I did manage to get him inside through the window because I was pretty worried about the little fellow. I went into the kitchen to get him a drink of water and offered it to him, but he wouldn't even blink at me. I sat the water on the table beside my bed and then he told me that he seen it.

He told me that he had seen a ghost as sure as the world. He told me that he got to the house before sundown and crawled through a side window that had the glass broken out. He was in there just walking from room to room, just looking around, and nothing scary happened at all.

He thought he was going to be all right when suddenly he heard a voice saying for him to get out. He looked around and seen a shadow in the middle of the room, and he could smell a terrible smell. Now, a terrible smell like that when seeing a shadow either means he is looking at a demon or he has done and gassed his pants something fierce.

He said he has never been so scared in all of his life, and I tell you I haven't been so scared in my life listening to someone who said they've never been so scared in theirs.

When he saw that shadow, he told me he ran out of that house as fast as he could, and he didn't stop running until he got here.

I asked what I thought to be a very important question. "You didn't bring that thing here did you?"

His eyes widened, but then he said he outran it for sure. He seemed to talk himself into it, and then he told me to smell the air if I didn't believe him, because when he saw that ghost he smelled sulfur for sure.

So I took me a big whiff and I didn't smell a ghost, though his stick smelled a little funny, but I guessed we were in the clear.

Billy stayed the night lying on the floor in my room with his stick in his hands, and neither of us slept a wink. Every little noise that we heard scared us to death, and then I got to worrying that Billy might mistake me for a ghost and swat me with his stick.

But the good Lord kept us safe through the night, and we made it to sunrise ghost-free. I tell you the sight of the sun coming up was one of the most wonderful things me and Billy had ever seen in our lives.

Even though Billy did run away, I think he did prove himself, and I for one think he was mighty brave to at least try and spend the night in that haunted house.

CHAPTER
ELEVEN

GOODBYE JUNIOR

Mary's got Junior problems. She caught him looking at that Virginia June girl when he should have been looking at her, and all fire broke loose.

Why, shoot, I look at that Virginia June girl, too, because she's as pretty as she can be, but with the way Mary acted I don't think I'd ever do it in front of her. To Mary, Virginia is that "Trashy thing that has the morals of a dish rag."

I don't really know what that means, but if Virginia June is a dish rag then I pray that God will turn me into a cup and a saucer.

Junior came over today to try and get Mary unmad. If he can do that the rest of the family would be very happy, because she has been a real pain here lately. When she gets mad, she goes completely insane. She'll yell at you and then cry and then yell at you for making her cry and then cry for making her yell.

When Junior came over, him and Mary sat in the living room, and Mommy went upstairs to do her sewing so they could work things out between them. Me and my sissies stood at the top of the stairs and listened.

We couldn't hear anything Junior said, but we could hear everything Mary said. Everyone in London, England, both living and dead, heard everything Mary said.

She yelled, "Are you running with me or are you running with Virginia June?" Junior tried to say he was running with her, but she wouldn't even let him answer the questions she was asking him.

Me and my sissies couldn't help but laugh. I think it would have been less painful for Junior if he just had her shoot him dead and got the whole thing over with.

Mommy came out and told us to go outside and play and let Mary and Junior tend to their problems, so we all ran down the stairs laughing and giggling as we passed by the two lovers.

Outside, we seen a frog jumping around the front yard and Suzie let out a scream, but Sally ran over and picked it up. Sally began teasing Suzie with it before letting it go.

About that time, Junior came marching out of the house with Mary screaming at him that she didn't want to ever see him again. He said she didn't have to worry about that and told her right then and there that he was an independent man and he didn't need to be yelled at all the time. He said he was going to go through this world alone and like every minute of it and that he didn't need the help of anyone because he was a man and he would do as he pleased.

He then went over to his daddy, who had drove him there, and they got into his daddy's truck and they drove off and the frog went under the porch.

CHAPTER TWELVE

LOTS OF ADVENTURE TODAY

I went to the Henderson farm down the road to take the horse blanket Mommy sewed for them, and when I got there, I seen that they had them a brand-new horse.

I had never ridden a horse before. Well, I sat on a pony one time. It didn't move or anything. I tried to get it to move, but it just stood there and ate grass the whole time. When I got off of it, I ripped the seat of my pants and had to run inside with my hands over my butt so no one could see. That was the sum total of my horse-riding experience.

Mr. Henderson seen me looking at his new horse, and I reckon he thought I ought to ride it. I don't know why he thought it, but I was sure glad he did. I went over to Henry - that's the horse's name - and I was both scared and excited at the same time.

Mr. Henderson held the horse for me by a rope that was tied around his head, and I petted it a couple times and asked him how he was and if he had been having a good time here at the Henderson farm. You know, just horse talk. Mr. Henderson told me to go ahead and get on it, but I didn't have the slightest idea how I was going to do that; it was much too tall for me to hope to get up on without a saddle. So he took Henry over to the fence, and I got up on top of the fence post and was able to get on top of the horse.

Mr. Henderson began leading it around the yard, and I was actually riding a horse! It was a great feeling. I must have been on the thing for about half an hour, and when I finally did get off, I'm proud to say that I didn't rip my pants.

When I got back home, there was some people there that I had never seen. It turns out that Mary was going to start giving piano lessons today. This was something her and Mommy talked about, and me, Sally, and Suzie had no idea this was coming at us. Now, I have to say that Mary is real good at pianoing. However, her students are not. When they play, they sound like they're strangling something.

Mary and Mommy are the only ones that can play the thing. Mommy tried to teach all of us how to piano right, but Mary was the only one that really caught on.

Mary has three students, all girls, as if I don't have enough women circulating through these parts. While they did their playing, I went and done me some fishing. With money as tight as it is, I can't fish for pleasure. I have to catch something so we'll have something to eat for supper.

It does make me feel good to bring a mess of fish home because it means I'm doing my part to help the family. Mommy fixed it for supper and it was good. I sometimes wonder what we would do if I came home empty-handed.

Oh, and when I got back from my fishing I had my first day of chopping wood. I was terrible at it, too. I was scared of the ax, to start with, then when I went to chop it I would miss the wood or just skim the edge, sending it flying through the air.

One piece of wood hit the side of the house, and that's a good fifty feet away. Mommy came out and told me to put that ax down before I killed myself or knocked the house down.

I put it down, but I think as the only man - well, boy may be a better word - I should have to cut the wood. At least that's how I feel.

That night came the wildest storm there ever was. It started about midnight and seemed to get stronger and stronger with each minute that went by.

One big, loud roar of thunder came one time, and me and my sissies ran into each other in the hallway trying to get into Mommy's room. I mean, the whole house shook with that thunderbolt.

We all piled into Mommy's bed, scared to death. She said that she had been expecting us and was wondering what took us so long. That wind got strong and Suzie and Sally thought they heard a tornado outside.

Mommy said there wasn't no tornado out there and we were letting our imaginations run away with us. She said that we should sing something to try and get our minds off of the storm, and I got a little worried that the piano might come into the picture, but thankfully we sung without any musical accompaniment.

Mary began singing "Joy to the World," and we all joined in. By the time we got to the part where heaven and nature sings, a loud thunder clap hit and shook the house from top to bottom again. I even felt my teeth rattle.

I just knew that lightning had hit the house, but Mommy said it would be okay and that she had been through worse when she was a little girl. She said she once seen it rain cats and dogs and hogs and frogs. We laughed and told her that was impossible. She said it was true and that the whole town had to eat bacon and frog legs three times a day for a whole year to clean up the mess. We asked her what they did with the cats and dogs and she said they was good, too.

We laughed, and Sally laughed so much she snorted, which made us all laugh more. About three in the morning, the storm died down and it was safe enough for us to go back to our own beds, but we stayed right in there with Mommy. I don't know about my sissies, but I slept just fine. Mommies are always good to sleep with when you're scared.

CHAPTER
THIRTEEN

THE NEW PIANO STUDENT

As Mary was giving her piano lessons, I sat in the kitchen with my hands over my ears, and I dare say in more pain than any boy should be allowed to go through. If I have to listen to them doing their pianoing much longer, I may become deranged enough to try and strangle something.

They hit the same bad note every time and play it over and over and over again. Why, if I was Mary, I would be too afraid to let anyone know I was their teacher because if other parents heard 'em playing, I would never get another student again. So I thought I better get out of the house right now.

Well, when I got to the door, guess who I saw? It was Billy. But Billy didn't look like Billy. He was all dressed up and even had his hair combed with a part right down the middle of his bright-red hair.

It seemed a little odd to be dressed up in the middle of the week, but I was just glad to see a fellow around instead of a bunch of girls and asked him if he wanted to go fishing. He said he couldn't, and I asked him why he couldn't, and he told me because it was time for his piano lesson.

I says, "Piano lessons? Are you crazy? Just listen to 'em in there."

Poor Billy thought they were just tuning the thing to play and I had to tell him that it was actually the sounds of what they are being taught.

I thought I might as well bring him in, and he followed me into what we call the piano room, though I refer to it as the torture chamber.

The little girl that was playing stopped, and her mother told her how proud of her she was and they left. I have to say that the silence that followed was joyous beyond belief.

Then I told Mary that her star pupil had arrived, which made Billy laugh. About that time Sally came running down the stairs with her fishing pole and noticed Billy sitting there all gussied up.

"Hi, Billy," she says. "You look pretty."

When she said that, Billy's face turned redder than his hair.

I said, "Boys aren't pretty. They're supposed to be handsome. If boys look pretty then they've done something wrong."

Mary then said, "I think Billy looks very handsome."

Billy grinned from ear to ear.

Then Sally asked Billy, "Do you want to go fishing?"

I told her that he had to have his piano lesson first, and a look came on her face like she thought he had done and gone the way of the rabbit.

Then she told him that he would have a better time fishing, but he would have none of it. He then gave Mary his dime and he said he would come by and check on our fishing after his lesson.

So Sally and me went outside and headed over to the wood house so I could fetch my pole. As we made our way back by the house, we heard some of the most beautiful piano music that we had ever heard.

Me and Sally looked through the window into the piano room, and do you know what we seen? It was Billy sawing on that piano like he done and knew what he was doing! When he got through with his playing, me and Sally started to clap.

Billy seen us in front of the window and stood up and bowed to us, which caused him to knock over a glass of water and all of his sheet music fell on the floor.

I asked him how he ever learned to do that, and he said he was taught by his aunt back before she died. I asked how she died, and Mary scolded me and told me I shouldn't be asking something like that. But Billy answered it anyway and said she had fallen out of a window while dancing. I asked if the fellow she was dancing with fell on her when they went out the window, and he said she was dancing by herself and must have got too close to the window. He then said that she was a very enthusiastic dancer.

None of us really knew what to say to that.

Then I told him he was a good piano player, and Sally told him that she didn't even know that our piano could make sounds like that.

Mary was bragging on him, too. Then me and Sally headed out to the river to catch us some fish.

After which one odd thing really stood out to me. The whole time me and Sally were fishing, Sally was quiet, and Sally doesn't do anything quiet. In fact, any time a girl goes a long time without talking, that is the number one sign that they are up to no good.

Billy came by later and seen how we were doing. We showed him the two trout we caught, and then we bragged on his piano playing some more and you could tell he liked to be bragged on.

He told me that today was the first time he can recall where he came over to my house and nothing bad happened. Then fate took over and he slipped and fell into the river. Me and Sally quickly fished him out and he stood there all soggy in his best clothes. He said he'll probably get switched for it, so if we heard any screaming later on for us not to worry because it was just him on the wrong end of the discussion with his mommy.

That Billy sure is something.

CHAPTER FOURTEEN

BILLY'S SECRET

Me and Billy went walking up in the mountains behind the house today. We decided to go up to the log cabin up on top. We don't know who built it or why, but it's been there as long as I've been living.

There's no sign that anyone has ever lived in it, so I don't know what it was built for. It's got a cutout opening for a doorway but no door. Some cutouts for windows but no windows. And a roof made of tin. The logs are square and gray and giant. Some of them are twenty-four inches wide. On the inside it has a wood-plank floor and a back porch that overlooks the mountains.

It takes a pretty good hike up a steep hill to get to it, and we had to stop a few times to rest, but then we got to going again. When me and Billy finally got up to it, we were sure happy it wasn't any farther up the mountain or we might not have made it.

We went inside the cabin and began looking around. Suddenly we heard some sort of buzzing noise. We didn't know what it was or where it was coming from, but then Billy shouted, "Hornets!"

Billy and I ran toward the door as fast as we could, and that's when we came to the realization that two boys, side by side, couldn't fit through that doorway. Our shoulders hit, causing me to bite my tongue, and Billy flew one way into the right wall and I flew the other way into the left wall.

This was just great, I thought. We're trying to get away from being stung to death and we almost knocked each other out cold.

Well, we finally got back up and headed out the door and stood outside trying to figure out what to do. That's when we seen the nest hanging down from the roof rafter on the other side. It was a big one, about the size of a watermelon. I'm talking about the size of a Fourth of July watermelon, too. Not one of them late-in-the-year ones nobody wants.

We decided we best not hang around there too much or else we'd be stung for sure. It was a little depressing to walk and crawl all that way up the mountain only to have to turn around and head back down.

After a bit of walking down the mountain we both got mighty hot and thirsty. We stopped at a stream and got us a drink and just sat there and talked while we cooled off.

That's when Billy said, "I have to tell you something and I don't want you to tell anybody else in the whole world."

"Okay," I said, not having any idea what he was going to spring on me because he looked dead serious.

He said, "You can't tell anyone even if you're tied up and set on fire or even if someone was going to force you to swim across the river with tractor tires tied to your arms."

I said, "Can't I just promise to hope to die instead?"

"No," he said.

"Okay," I told him.

"You promise not to tell anyone?" he asked me again.

"For crying out loud, Billy," I said. "What is it?"

"I like Suzie," he said.

"That's it?" I shouted. "That's your big secret that you want me tortured to death for? Everybody in my family knows that you like Suzie!"

That's when he began yelling that I had told them and he had thought I was his friend. Then he said I was a blabbermouth just like a girl.

Being called a blabbermouth just like a girl kind of cuts a fellow pretty deep. So I reminded him, "You fainted in front of her! So I didn't tell her you liked her, you did!" I have to admit that my voice got a little high when I said that, too.

He stood up and told me that I sure can't keep a secret, and he took off and I had to hurry to catch up to him. It was a few minutes that passed before he decided he could talk to me again. I guess he got curious.

"What did Suzie say when you told her that I liked her?"

"Well, I didn't exactly tell Suzie straight out. I told Sally and then Suzie overheard what I was telling because she was standing right there while I was doing my telling," I told him.

"Then what happened?"

"She ran away crying."

Billy stared at me, stunned.

"Ran away crying? Why did she do that for?"

"Girls are just an odd species."

"I have done and fallen in love with the wrong girl, haven't I?" Billy asked.

"Well, you got to remember that you had fainted in front of her, and Sally said you was dead. Then that meant that Suzie had killed you, and that's why she ran away crying. When you think about it that way, it makes some sense."

His expression began changing from hurt to happy.

"Hey, wait a minute now. This could be a good sign. She cried because she thought she had killed me."

"Yeah."

"That has to mean that she has some feelings for me. I mean, people die all the time, but I don't cry over them. So she has to like me a little. You know what I think? I think that deep down her crying shows that she wants to marry me."

"Well, I think she was more feared that if she had killed you that she might end up in jail, but you could be right. You can't really tell with girls."

He thought it over a bit and said, "I like my version better than the fearing-jail version."

I have to confess that his version was a little more romantic, but I couldn't convince him none that he may be putting a little too much into her crying. In fact, I think I'd have a bctter chancc talking with them hornets than trying to get Billy to understand that Suzie didn't really love him.

"I'm going to do it," he said. "You have given me the courage to do something that I couldn't do on my own. I'm going to ask Suzie to be my girl."

"What happens if she says no?" I asked.

He was quiet for a few seconds and then said, "Sometimes in life you have to go on faith. A man has to try, and try I will."

So down the mountain we went, and I couldn't keep up with him at all. He had love on the brain and foot, and he was determined to see it through.

We got down to part of the hill that overlooked the house, and we both seen Suzie outside on the tire swing that was roped around the oak tree.

I turned to Billy and said, "Fate is on a tire swing."

But when I turned around, do you know what I saw? Billy running as far away from Suzie as he could get.

I guess he had done and lost his nerve. Perhaps in the end love is better from afar than facing it on a tire swing.

You'd think that a boy that stayed in a haunted house and got stuck in bat poop wouldn't be afraid of a girl, but running away don't lie.

CHAPTER
FIFTEEN

THE GRAVE AND THE BEAR

Today, Mommy, me, and my sissies went over to where my daddy is buried. Mommy put some flowers on the grave and stood quiet for a long time, and it looked like even a tear started rolling down her face. I found the whole thing depressing more than anything else. No boy wants to see his mommy cry.

It's kind of strange for me to visit my daddy's grave because I don't know anything about him. Why, we don't even have a photo of him, so I don't even know what he looks like. All I know is that visiting his grave makes my mommy sad, so I always hate going to it.

While Mommy tended to the gravesite, picking weeds and such, I went over to the fence that was around the graveyard and noticed about a zillion ants running up and down the post.

I don't know why I was so interested in them, I mean they're just ants, but watching 'em got me to thinking almost like a writer. I, for reasons unknown to me, wrote me my very first poem, and it was about these ants, so I thought I'd write it down in my journal here like Mrs. Collins told me I should do. But don't laugh.

Ants! Ants!
Working all day long.
Doing their job
from sun near to sun gone.
Hunting and gathering
for the oncoming winter
so when the snow falls
they would be eating their dinner.

I kind of liked it. I started another journal for my poems and wrote several of them, but it seems like the "Ants" one was the best. I also learned when I was writing a different poem that it's kind of hard to find a word that rhymes with zebra.

Billy told me a joke yesterday, and I thought that I would write it down because I remembered how Mrs. Collins told me that I could put jokes down in my journal, too. You're allowed to laugh at this one.

Why did the cow jump over the moon? Because it wouldn't mooooove.

Billy laughed so hard when he told me this that his face got real red. Why, he even cracked up before he could get to the ending of the joke, which made me laugh more at the way he was telling it than the actual joke itself.

That evening as I was eating supper, I heard something on the outside. I looked up at Mommy, who must have heard it at the same time that I did.

Mommy got up and went over to the kitchen window and yelled, "Land sakes alive!"

Me and my sissies got up from the table as fast as we could and looked out that window and seen us a black bear roaming around the yard. Why, the thing even walked up on the front porch! Which made Mommy run to the front door and lock it while Mary ran around the kitchen table to lock the back door.

I don't really know if that would have helped any because the bear wouldn't use the doorknob to open the door.

We watched the bear walk around outside until it would disappear from sight and we'd hurry to another room and look out that window to see if we could see it again. It was exciting as could be.

We couldn't call anybody because we don't have a phone, but after about twenty minutes I reckon it got tired of our place and went on off into the woods.

Mommy thought it might have come down from the mountains looking for some food from the fallen trees of the storm we had the other night. So she made me and my sissies pick up all the fallen branches in the yard, and she got a lot of junk she wanted to get rid of, and we made us a big pile of it in the backyard. Then when it got dark, Mommy lit it all on fire and we had us a big time.

That fire burnt red hot, but we were clear of all the other woods and the house so nothing could catch on fire. When we all went back in the house after the fire burnt down, we all noticed that all our faces was as red as could be from the heat of the fire.

But we sure had a good time.

CHAPTER SIXTEEN

SUNDAY

I'm sitting on the hill above my house as I write this. My mommy has gone into town to sell some more of her clothes and blankets and to get some new sewing jobs.

The people in town give Wart - he's the man that owns the store and is Junior's daddy - their requests or things that they want sewn, and Mommy comes in on Saturday and drops off last week's work and picks up another week's work to take home. She had a little extra to do on this sewing and finished it up last night and decided to take it on in today.

I also learned today that Wart's name is Mr. Henry. Well, I don't know if that's his first name or last name, but Mommy told me to call him that. She just wasn't comfortable calling him Wart all the time.

The people Mommy sews for leave the money with Mr. Henry, and then he pays Mommy and she uses that money to buy the things we need. My sissies are real good at sewing, too, so they help out Mommy a lot.

I thought since I was up here looking down at my house that I would describe it for anyone that might one day read this. It is made of wood planks, painted white, with a tin roof. It has a front porch, but no back porch. All it has at the back door is a flat stone for a step. We have running water from our well that runs into the kitchen, and underneath the kitchen in the basement is the shower. However, it doesn't have any hot water, so if you want a hot shower, you have to heat the water in a bucket on top of the stove in the kitchen and then tote it down into the basement and pour it over your head. All our showers, hot or cold, are real quick.

We do have electricity. It gets hard for Mommy to pay for sometimes and they shut it off for a while until we get the bill paid, but they haven't shut it off one time this year.

The house has a kitchen, a living room/piano room, three bedrooms, two downstairs and one upstairs, an attic, and the basement. Mommy says that my bedroom and the bedroom of my sissies used to be a side porch that Daddy closed in and divided up and made two bedrooms out of it. Mommy's bedroom is the one upstairs.

The attic is real small and serves as a junk place. The only thing of any value in the attic is the fishing pole that Sally keeps up there. I keep my fishing pole out in the wood house, but Sally thinks it's too snaky out there.

We don't go to church no more because the place where we was going got a woman preacher, and Mommy don't cotton to women preaching. But Mommy reads the Bible to us every night before we go to bed. It seems to be more important to her than it does to me, but I guess I'll look at it different when I get older.

But if Mommy wants to read the Bible to me before I go to bed, then that's all right with me.

Then after she reads a chapter we have our prayers. We all pray out loud in turns from the oldest to the youngest. I usually pray the same thing every night, for God to watch over Mommy and my sissies and to watch over Billy, and I ask for a dog.

I wonder if I keep praying the same thing every night will God even listen to me anymore. I mean what I pray. I want God to watch over the people I'm praying for, but I don't know what else to say. I'm embarrassed to admit that sometimes my mind will even wander when I'm praying, and I up and forget what I was praying about.

When we get finished with our praying, we all head out the back door to the outhouse. Mommy gets a candle we have that Mary calls our magic candle, which we use all the time for our nightly outhouse visits - until it burns gone, then we'll get another magic candle to use all of the time. We sometimes sing our outhouse song. Mommy said it was the same song that she sung when she was little.

Going to the outhouse
all day long.
Having fun
singing my song.
From me to God
this prayer I send.
Please dear Lord
don't let me fall in.

It looks a lot dumber on paper than it feels when singing it, but I guess everyone has strange things in their lives that they do. It just so happens that ours occurs while going to the toilet.

CHAPTER
SEVENTEEN

MY FIRST COMIC BOOK

Me and Sally was counting the number of cars on the train that went by this morning and counted a hundred six. That's not the most we have ever counted, for we once seen a hundred ninety-five cars, and it had two engines pulling it.

After that I figured it was about time for Billy's piano lesson to be over for the day, so me and Sally then went back to the house and seen, much to our surprise, that Mommy was on top of the roof.

Sally thought maybe all of that piano playing from Mary's students had finally got to Mommy and she had up and gone crazy.

We asked her, "Why are you on the roof for?"

"I'm trying to fix a leak!" she shouted down at us.

She said that she had found it while trying to kill a mouse with her broom in the attic. The mouse got away, but the leak didn't. So she was up there hammering away trying to fix the thing. I was a little nervous watching her, but she didn't seem scared none.

She had built her ladder out of some old lumber that washed up on the riverbank after a flood last summer. She's real handy to have around, but a boy still doesn't like to see his mother up on the roof. After a bit, she deemed it good and climbed on down.

After Billy got done with his piano-playing lesson, we sat down beneath the oak tree that has the tire swing roped to it and he said, "I got something I want to show you."

He reached into his back pocket and pulled out a comic book. He showed me the cover and I just let out a great big "wow!"

It was about a man called Batman. I got to looking through it, and I think I must have said "wow!" about a million times. I asked him where he got it, and he said his granny sent him a bunch of comic books for a birthday present.

"A bunch of comic books? How many?" I asked him with more enthusiasm than I can ever remember having for something.

"Ten."

"Ten comic books!" I said. "She must love you to death."

"It beats socks," he told me, which may have been the biggest understatement ever uttered by a boy.

That's when I hit upon an idea.

"Hey, why don't we camp out here one night in the yard and you can bring all them comic books and we'll read 'em by the fire."

"Wow!" he said.

I asked my mommy if me and Billy could have us a campout in the yard, and she said she would have no trouble with it as long as Billy's parents said it was okay. So Billy ran home to ask and told me that he'd tell me tomorrow what they said.

Well, I sat under that oak tree all day long reading that comic book about a thousand times, then I'd stare at the pictures another thousand times. I took some of my old journal pages and began drawing me a Batman in the margins.

I tried to make it look like the Batman that was in the comic book, but I didn't do very good. Mine kept looking like he was going to fall over, so I gave up trying to draw it and went back to reading it again.

The next morning I was eating breakfast while looking at Billy's comic book when Sally came in and saw what I was reading.

"Where'd you get that?"

I told her, "Billy got it for his birthday, and he's going to bring the rest of them over and we're going to camp outside in the yard and read 'em by the fire."

Sally thought that was a great idea and wanted to camp out, too, but Mommy said girls can't camp out with boys because it wasn't proper. Sally said she wasn't trying to be proper, but Mommy told her no.

Mommy then said, "Price is surrounded by girls all day and night long. He needs to be able to have some boys over to where it's just them together."

I agreed, and Sally stayed mad at me and Mommy for the rest of the day.

CHAPTER
EIGHTEEN

THE CAMPOUT

Billy came over this morning and brought good news! He said that his folks said that he could camp with me tonight. So I went back with Billy to his house to help him carry his stuff to my house.

We got a box and put his comic books in it along with some blankets. We then toted that box back to my house, but before we got too far, Billy's mommy told him to come back and kiss her goodbye. Billy's face turned redder than a rose as he went back to kiss his mommy. I told him not to worry about it none because my mommy was the same way, though I did rib him a little. If best buddies didn't rib each other every now and then, they wouldn't be best buddies, they'd just be people.

We got back to my house and we put the box on the porch and we got to doing what boys are supposed to be doing - looking at them comic books. Me and Billy had them books all over the front porch when Mommy came out and told us that we should get us some wood if we were going to camp out. We guessed she was right, so we put the comic books back into the box and set out into the yard looking for the best place to set up our camp for the night.

After evaluating the yard, I decided the best place to set up our camp was over where we had burned all that brush the other day after that big storm. We could build us a fire there and not mess up anymore of the yard. Then we headed over to the wood house and started getting us some firewood.

Well, we got no more than one armload full of split-up firewood when Mommy came out and put a stop to that as fast as she could.

She said, "The wood in the wood house is for the house, not for you two to burn up while camping. If you want some firewood, you have to go out and get your own."

I didn't realize that camping out was going to take this much work. We had a box of comic books setting on the front porch not being read at all. But the law had spoken, so off into the woods me and Billy went looking for firewood. We gathered two loads each, and Billy thought that might be enough.

I said, "It ain't near enough, Billy! We want a fire to last all night, don't we?"

He said, "Yeah, but I don't want to spend all day getting it."

So off we went back into the woods and started picking up sticks, but I thought we needed something bigger. That's when I seen a log about six feet long and pretty big in thickness.

I told Billy, "Our problems have just been solved."

"What problems?" he asked.

"Getting firewood. Instead of getting small wood, which will take several loads, we'll just get one big log and then we're done."

Billy looked at the log that I put my foot on and he asked, "Do you think we can actually move that?"

"Of course we can. We're boys, ain't we?"

"I guess," said Billy.

"God made boys to move things. In fact, it's the number one reason boys get into trouble because they move things that weren't supposed to be moved in the first place. So, let's do our duty as boys and get to moving this log."

I told Billy to grab one end of the log and I grabbed ahold of the other, and we attempted to take it to our campsite.

Well, that thing must have weighed every bit of a ton, and we couldn't get it to move one inch.

Billy said, "God's going to have to send us some more boys, or we're going to have to just leave it here or hire Batman to come and get it for us."

"We can't leave it here because it's the perfect firewood log for camping," I said. "It would easily last all night and we'd be done getting firewood for the day and we could get back to them comic books."

So we stood there and studied about it for a bit. Billy came up with the idea of trying to roll it to the camp, but that didn't work. I got me a long stick and tried to pry it up, and I managed to get it up off the ground just a little and held it there not really knowing what the next part of my plan should actually be. So I had to let it down and Billy got mad.

"Why'd you let it back down for?"

"Because I didn't know what else to do with it!" I said in a rather loud voice.

So I looked at the log again pretty good and Billy looked at it pretty good, too, but in all honesty I don't think Billy knew what he was pretty gooding about.

Then I came up with a plan.

I told Billy, "If you ever find yourself in a situation in which something can't be moved, you go get an ax."

"When I find myself in a situation in which something can't be moved I just leave it be," Billy said.

I told him, "See, this is why we're camping out tonight. I have to reinforce your boyhood because you've done and let it go to waste. Boys don't leave stuff alone simply because it can't be moved. We either keep trying to move it until it does or pick at it until it bleeds."

"But what if we bleed?" asked Billy.

"Boys that don't bleed are called girls."

"I think we should just leave the log alone and just use it as a sitting log that we could come out to and set on and look at the woods. It would be nice to bring a girl out here, wouldn't it? Just sit here and talk to her."

With them words, Billy set back boyhood a million years.

I just ignored his words and I went to get the ax and came back over to the log and started swinging away at it. That's when I learned that if you want to chop something, the first thing you need is a pretty good aim. I kept having the handle just below the head of the ax hitting the log. In fact, it happened so much that it broke, and that caused me and Billy to become pretty concerned.

"We're going to die, aren't we?" Billy asked.

"We ain't gonna die, Billy."

"Your mommy is going to see that we broke her ax and beat us to death with the handle."

"She is not."

"So you're going to tell her what happened?"

"Do you think I'm crazy?"

"So she is going to kill us. I knew something would go wrong. Everything goes wrong when I'm involved. I'm a hoax. A full-blown hoax!"

"You mean jinx."

"I'm both of 'em tied in gravy. We're going to die, I just know it. I wish I was dead now just to get it over with."

"Would you just calm down?" I said. "I just meant that I wouldn't tell her about the ax right off. Because she might not let us camp out if I tell her now. We'll wait until morning after we've done our camping and you're safely back home, and then I'll tell her."

"I can't let your mommy kill you all alone. I was here with you when it happened so I should die, too."

"I appreciate that Billy, but sometimes it's best for a son to die alone than in front of his best buddy."

So we agreed to wait on telling Mommy, but that plan blew up in our faces when suddenly she was already on top of us.

"What are you two doing all the way up here?" she asked.

That's when she seen the ax handle in my hand and the ax head in Billy's hand.

"Don't kill us, Mrs. Mullins," said Billy.

"I'm not going to kill you, Billy," said Mommy. "How'd you break it?"

I told her that it was an accident and then Billy started crying. He kept saying that we didn't mean it and then he got down on his knees and hugged Mommy's legs saying, "Don't hang us in the woods!"

Mommy didn't know what Billy was talking about, and neither did I. She said she wasn't going to hang us in the woods, and wanted to know where he got a strange thought such as that.

Billy told her that Mary had said that you hang children in the woods if they don't practice their piano lessons every day. She told him that Mary was just pulling his leg and that she'd have a talk with her about that. Then she said that old ax handle was about to break anyway and we shouldn't worry about it none. She said she had gotten worried about us because she couldn't hear us, so she decided she better come and check on us to make sure we was still alive. Seeing that we were, she went on back to the house, and me and Billy went on to gathering us some smaller firewood.

After we spent a good long time gathering the firewood, we got some stones and made us a circle, and then we put some of the wood in the circle to get it ready to light once it got dark.

"I guess we're about ready for camping," Billy said.

"We need to get something to eat," I said.

"What?"

That's when I went and got my fishing pole, and we got ready to head down to the river to get us some fish for our campout. As we started off, it was no time before Sally came a-running after us carrying her fishing pole.

"Wait up!" she shouted.

"You can't come!" I shouted back.

"Why can't I?"

"Because it's just fellas that's allowed to go today."

"But I want to go, too," Sally said with a pouty mouth. "And you two don't get any say in the matter."

Then do you know what Billy done? He told Sally she could come with us. Told her right there in the daylight, too! I couldn't believe it.

I asked Billy, "Why did you do that for?"

"I thought it was the nice thing to do," he said, and he was grinning when he said it.

Sally agreed, and off the two of them went, leaving me standing there as mad as I've ever been at Billy in my life. It was just supposed to be me and him doing this and he invited not only another person, but somebody that was my own sister.

The whole time we was fishing, Billy and Sally talked and talked and talked. Then they'd start giggling and I started to steam.

"You all are going to scare all the fish away with your jabbering like that!"

But they didn't seem to care what I thought. What's worse is that Sally caught three trout, and all I caught was a green and white bread wrapper, and then I got my hook hung up in the branches in the tree up behind me, causing them to point and laugh at me, which made me madder than a wet hen.

It was not a good day to be Price Mullins, that is for dang tooting sure. In fact, I kind of got the feeling that Billy would rather spend the day with Sally than with me and his comic books.

Well, we all three got back to the house at about six in the evening, and Mommy was yelling at us for not getting back sooner for supper.

Billy bragged that Sally caught three trout and then had to say that I caught a tree. Mommy laughed, Billy laughed, Mary laughed, Sally laughed, and Suzie laughed. I, on the other hand, just wanted to start the campfire and get to our camping and reading comic books and get as far away from women folk as I possibly could.

Then if I wasn't humiliated enough, Mommy wouldn't let me start the campfire because she was afraid I might get burned. I couldn't believe this was happening to me, and right here in front of Billy, too. This was an embarrassment of the highest proportions. Women folk just don't understand what being a boy is supposed to be. When a fella camps out in the woods, I know of no time when he brings his mommy along with him to start his fires for him.

But the fire got going and I guess in the end that's the goal. Mommy took Sally's trout inside and said we could have them for breakfast and that we could eat the supper she fixed out here by the fire. So we had chicken and taters with buttermilk for our campfire supper.

After we got done eating and it got dark, every one of my sissies came out and sat with us. I told them they needed to go back inside because me and Billy was doing our camping, but they said they wanted to hang around the fire.

I wasn't too happy about it, but Billy didn't seem to mind at all. In fact, I'd say he liked my sissies being out with us pretty good. *Too* pretty good, if you ask me.

Finally my sissies decided to go back in, and Billy wanted to know if they wanted to camp out with us. I told Billy they couldn't camp out with us because they was girls and we was boys and then I just said it:

"Billy, it is high time you decided whose side you're on! Are you on my side or are you on the side of my sissies?"

Everything got quiet. The first time all day, actually. Billy said he was on my side and he didn't mean anything by it. He was just trying to be nice, is all.

Then Mary whispered something to my other sissies, and they all started to giggle, which is never a good sign. That's when disaster struck. All three of them came over and kissed Billy right on the jaw and told him good night.

Billy's face got red, but he was grinning bigger than I ever saw him grin before. My sissies went back in, and Billy just stared at me and said, "I have never been kissed by a girl in my whole life, and on this night I was kissed by three of them at one time. Pretty ones, too."

He sighed, and I knew at that very moment that he had done and gone over to the other side.

But the night was still early, and we had some serious comic book reading to get to, so we had at it.

I told Billy that Batman could beat up anybody in the world, but Billy said he couldn't beat up Superman.

I didn't know who Superman was and didn't really care because I am now a Batman man, and when you become a Batman man, that means no one can beat your fella up.

Billy said Superman could fly and he was built like steel. He could pick cars up over his head and run faster than a train. Nothing could stop him but kryptonite.

I told him I'd have to see that to believe it. Billy said he didn't have any Superman comic books, but he read one at the store. I told him that I still think that Batman can beat up Superman while blindfolded and with a bad case of gas, which made Billy laugh.

We looked at those comic books just about all night long. We also talked about a lot of different things.

I told him there was something in my life I would like to be able to do before I died. Billy wanted to know what it was, and I told him I'd like to see me one of them moving pictures.

Billy said he'd like to see one, too, but his mommy wouldn't let him because she thought movies was full of sinning and such, and it wasn't a place for a little boy, or a big boy for that matter, to go to and watch.

I told Billy that I haven't seen a moving picture because we don't have enough money to go see one. It never dawned on me about that sin thing.

Billy said he seen that the movie *Jesse James* was playing down at the movie palace this week, and he had seen them put up the poster in the window for it. He said it starred Henry Fonda, but neither of us knew who that was. But we both would have sure liked to have seen that picture.

We then laid out on our blankets and looked up into the sky and wondered how many stars is up there looking down on us. Billy said it was probably millions. I asked him how millions would look if it was on the ground, and he said it would look like tons.

I guess Billy knows what he's talking about. He's a lot smarter than me when it comes to book learning. Of course, everyone is a lot smarter than me when it comes to book learning.

I asked Billy if he thought one day people would walk on the moon and he said he didn't think so. I said why and he said it was too far. I thought you could just fly a plane up there and land it and run around and start shouting, "I'm on the moon!"

That's when he told me that there wasn't any air on the moon, and if anyone went there they'd die because air was one of the basic food groups. I didn't know that.

That's when our talking turned to Billy's daddy's milk cow. When Billy's daddy was a little daddy, his family owned a milk cow and it was always trying to get into the house like cat, so they called it Kitty. Then he told me that Kitty once got her head hung up between two trees, and they had to saw one of the trees down to get her out. He then told me how his daddy used to ride Kitty around the yard like a horse, and then he asked me if I ever rode a horse. I told him twice, but I didn't mention about me ripping my pants.

I asked him whatever happened to Kitty, and he told me that she died of old age. He said they even buried her. I thought that was very interesting. It probably took a long time to bury a cow.

I guess we then fell asleep. When you start talking about burying a cow, you have pretty much used up all the conversation for the day.

CHAPTER NINETEEN

JUNIOR AND CRAWDADS

Billy went on home this morning, and he said he had him a good ol' time camping out with me. He left his box of comics with me to look at, so I was pretty happy about that.

A little later, me and Sally went down to the river with a bucket to catch us some crawdads. I would lift up the rocks and see if any were under there, and Sally would stand on the riverbank with the bucket. When I found one, I'd take it over to where Sally was standing and dropped it in.

Sally hates crawdads. Well, she likes to eat 'em, but she hates the way they look. She said they give her the "creepies." That seems a little odd coming from her since she really had no trouble with worms when she baited her fishing hook and such, but I guess if that Superman fella can have a weakness, then so can we. It's just that Sally's kryptonite is crawdads.

It took awhile before I found any, but then I found three pretty easy. One of them I had to put back because it was too small. I did find a big one, and I told Sally that I was going to eat it. I put it in the bucket and went back into the water. I had my pant legs rolled up with my shoes on the side of the riverbank when Sally began laughing.

I said, "What are you laughing for?"

She said, "An orange salamander just crawled into your shoe. Now you'll have salamander stink on your feet."

"Get it out for me," I hollered back at her.

"I ain't touching it. My hands would have salamander stink on it."

But she did finally pick up my shoe and turned it upside down for the salamander to fall out. Only thing was, it didn't fall out. So she began shaking the shoe real hard and then swinging it from side to side to try and get that little fellow out of there. Well, it finally came out, but not the way Sally was fixing for it to. It flew way up in the air and landed in her hair belly side up.

I don't believe I have ever heard such screaming in all of my days. She started beating on her head to try and get it out of her hair, and I started laughing, which made her madder than a hornet. In fact, I think I made her a little too mad because she picked up both of my shoes and threw them into the river about as far as she could throw 'em.

"What are you doing, you crazy woman?" I shouted.

"That'll teach you not to laugh at me!" she shouted back at me with her hands on her hips and her lips all puckered out as if she was something big.

So I had to go fetch my blasted shoes out of the river before they floated away. She stayed angry for the rest of the time until I fell face first into the river looking for crawdads. That made her laugh and helped her get over her mad spell. It, however, did nothing for me.

We caught us sixteen crawdads and then headed back home.

A little later while I was lying in the middle of the yard letting my clothes dry, I heard a truck pull up. I got to looking and seen it was Junior. He got out of his truck and came over to where I was.

"What are you doing?" he asked.

"I'm drying my clothes."

He stared at me kind of awkward-like and asked me if I was okay. I told him that I was. I talked to him about Batman and how me and Billy camped out last night. He didn't really pay too much attention to what I was saying.

He asked, "Is Mary here?"

I told him, "Yep."

"What's she doing?"

"She's teaching piano right now to some of the worst piano players in these parts."

I figured he'd known that because you could hear that bad piano playing from ten miles away. Mommy then came out onto the porch and told Junior howdy and Junior howdyed back, and Mommy went back inside and suddenly the piano playing stopped.

That's when Mary came out onto the porch and sort of just stood there. Junior walked over toward the porch and I went somewhere else to dry my pants.

When I was walking around, I found a turtle by the wood house. As soon as I picked it up, it pulled its head back into its shell. Suzie and Sally came out to where I was and wanted to know if I had dried off yet. I told ‘em I did and then showed ‘em the turtle.

Suzie asked, “Why’s it in its shell for?”

“He’s afraid we’re going to eat it,” Sally said.

“I don’t think I could eat a turtle. They just don’t look that good to me,” said Suzie. “They’re old-looking and all wrinkly. It would be like eating grandpa’s toes.”

Then the three of us just went walking around the house to see what we could get into without getting a whipping. That’s when we ran into Junior leaned up against the house like he was holding it up.

“What are you doing out here, Junior?” Sally asked.

“I was waiting for Mary to finish her piano lessons.”

“Are you two getting back together?” Sally asked.

He just smiled and humped his shoulders. I guess their getting back together is more up to Mary than to him.

That’s when I looked down and seen a bunch of ants all over a dragonfly. They were carrying it on their backs. I got down on my knees to take a closer gander at them, and Suzie and Sally got down to have a closer look themselves.

“That is just plain old filthiness right there,” Suzie said.

“I wonder what a dragonfly would taste like,” Sally said.

Junior told her that this was her chance to find out.

That’s when she yelled that she wasn’t going to eat it, and I told her she was chicken. Suzie then told me to eat it and I said I wasn’t going to, and then all three of them called me chicken. I said I wasn’t no chicken, and before I knew it I had done and grabbed ahold of that dragonfly, ants and all, and put it in my mouth.

Junior started laughing, and Sally and Suzie stared at me with horror on their faces. I truly believed that my tongue had the same kind of horror all over it as their faces did.

I spit the dragonfly out right quick, and Junior wanted to know what it tasted like.

"A lot like you think it would," I said.

As I looked back on the incident, I think I was pretty brave to put an ant-covered dragonfly in my mouth. And in doing so I proved I ain't chicken.

I can't wait to tell Billy.

CHAPTER TWENTY

THE BASEBALL

It was the middle of the day when I decided to head on out to Billy's to see what he was up to. I got about halfway there when you know what I saw? I saw that Billy coming up the road heading for my house to see what I was up to.

Billy said he's been hoeing the garden all morning, and he was pretty glad to be just about anywhere as long as it wasn't in peas. He said he got a blister on his hand and his back hurts.

I told him I ate a dragonfly and he wanted to know what I did that for, and I told him because I had to prove that I wasn't chicken. Billy said that they would have had to do a whole lot more to him than call him chicken to get him to eat a dragonfly. I told him I sort of did it without thinking, and he said he hoped so. In all honesty, he didn't seem as impressed with my putting a dragonfly in my mouth as I wanted him to be. But

I guess when you think about it, putting a dragonfly in your mouth wasn't one of my best life choices.

Me and Billy walked down to the river to see if we might find something. A lot of junk washed along the riverbank after storms, and we'd had a big one recently, and this time I found something great.

It was wedged between two rocks, and I couldn't believe what I was seeing. But it was apparent that God had decided this was the day that Price Mullins will remember for the rest of his life.

I didn't tell Billy at first until I was sure that it was really what I thought it was. I went over to it and picked it up, and it sure was what I thought it was. I yelled for Billy and told him I found something better than gold.

Billy came running over and I showed him. It was a baseball. A real-life baseball. Billy got so excited that he couldn't even see straight and kept saying "Oh, man" so many times that it got on my nerves and I told him to quit it.

We sat down on a rock beside the river and took turns holding that baseball. Neither of us had held a real baseball before, and we couldn't believe this was happening. We both had played baseball at school, but we used a can as the ball. But this was the real deal.

The baseball had a gash in it and it was waterlogged, but other than that it was in perfect shape. We decided to take it back to my place and let it dry out. We took turns carrying it. Why, we treated that baseball like it was a newborn baby. We even talked to the thing. I know most people might think that's sort of weird, but if you're a boy, you'll fully understand.

Billy then got to wondering how it got in the river. I told him maybe someone hit a home run somewhere and it landed in the river and floated downstream until it got stuck back there. Billy thought maybe it was a sign from on high that we're supposed to be big league ballplayers when we grow up.

I said I didn't know about that, but it could be possible. After all, anybody could have found that baseball, but not just anybody did - me and Billy did, and I don't think you can look over that important fact.

We got to my house and we sat it on a rock near the wood house to dry some more. We then sat on the ground near it and watched it. Watching that baseball dry was one of the most exciting things I have ever done in my life. Thoughts of playing with it came rushing through my mind, and I could see all the glory that would create. Finally me and Billy could watch that thing of beauty dry no more. A baseball was made for playing with and not for watching.

I told Billy to go stand over there by the stump and I'd throw it to him. So Billy went over there and my day of destiny had arrived. I was about to throw a baseball! I looked at that baseball in my hand and then I looked at Billy. I then took my arm and threw that baseball and it proceeded to go over top of Billy's head by a good twenty feet. It then went rolling and bouncing along the ground and disappeared into some thorn bushes and thick brush in the woods.

Me and Billy stopped at the edge of the woods and just looked around in horror. I thought I was going to cry. I couldn't believe it. Destiny had given me a baseball and I lost it in the thorn bush behind the house.

I tried crawling into that bush, but the thorns were sharper than a snake's tooth. This got me so mad I thought I was going to - well, I don't know exactly what I was going to do. Billy tried to encourage me and said maybe we can get it in the fall when the briars all die out. It would probably be dry by then, he said, but I told Billy no. We were going to get that baseball out of there right now even if I am thorned to death in the process. I was more determined at this moment than I have ever been in my life.

So I crawled onto the ground into the midst of them thorns, and Billy tried to keep 'em off of me the best he could, but there was too many of 'em. I could feel them things going clear through my clothes, but I didn't care. Well, actually I did care because it hurt like crazy, but I was going to see this through and rescue that there baseball.

I inched forward some into them thickets and I finally seen the baseball - it was up into them briars another three feet. I told Billy that I seen it and he told me that he knew I would find it. Then I tried to reach as far as I could, but it was no use, I couldn't reach it because them thorns were just too sharp for me.

I told Billy, "Run up to the wood house and get something so I can reach that baseball."

"What do I get?"

"I don't care, just get something."

"How about some fishing line?"

"That won't work!" I shouted.

"I thought it didn't matter what I got!" he shouted back.

"Billy," I said, "I am being stuck to death by these thorns. I don't have time to argue with you. Just get something rigid."

Then Billy took off, and I have to say it felt like that he was gone a good six days before he got back. Any movement I made sent another thorn into my back, but I was going to hold my position because my baseball was depending on me.

Then Billy came back carrying that ax handle that we had broke when we was chopping wood for our campout.

"Will this work?"

I said, "I think it will."

Billy gave me the handle and I slid it into the thicket and began rubbing that baseball with it and pushing it toward me as best as I could. Then I finally got it close enough to grab ahold of with my hand.

"I got it!"

"Hooray!" Billy cheered. "Batman would be proud of you."

I then managed my way out of the thorn bush and started dusting myself off. I told Billy, "I'll let you throw it this time."

"What if I break it?"

"You can't break it, it's made to be hit with a bat, for crying out loud. It's practically indestructible."

"I guess that's right."

So Billy took the baseball and I took my position in front of the wood house because I got to thinking that if it does go over my head, then the wood house would stop it from going any farther and we wouldn't lose it in the thorn bushes again.

Billy stood on that stump which he was at earlier. My heart began beating faster than it had ever beat before. I, Price Mullins, was about to catch a baseball!

He took a big windup and threw it as hard as he could. I put my hands up to snag that glorious object from the air when it went through my hands and busted me right in the mouth.

I fell backwards and hit my head on the wood house wall, and that ball came down after bouncing off the wood pile and landed right on top of me.

Billy came running over to me in fear that he had done and killed me. To be honest, I wasn't sure he hadn't.

I woozily asked Billy, "Where's the baseball?"

"It's laying on your stomach."

"You mean I swallowed it?" I asked him full of panic.

"No, it's *on* your stomach, not in it," Billy told me.

I felt a little better after that was cleared up.

My lip started to swell, and Billy said he was sorry and I told him it wasn't his fault and not to worry about it.

Billy helped me up and I held the baseball in my hand and I just kept staring at it. I didn't think it was possible for anything that was that small to cause so much trouble.

Billy then said we could use the ax handle as a bat. I thought that was a great idea. Maybe having a bat to defend myself against the baseball would be a good way to go. Billy went and stood about twenty feet away and he told me that he would toss it real easy this time. So Billy gave a gentle toss, and it didn't even get down to where I was standing.

I told him, "That has to be the sorriest throw in all of baseball history. You're going to have to throw it harder than that or run over here to me carrying it."

Billy said he would throw it harder, and he picked up the baseball and ran back to a piece of wood laying on the ground that he was using for a pitcher's mound. He threw the ball and it went behind me.

"For crying out loud, Billy, what are you doing?"

"I'm new at this, okay?"

"Do you want me to up and turn around?"

"No."

Billy ran and got the baseball and then assumed his position at his pitcher's mound. He looked at me, took a big windup, and threw it real hard at me. This time it was where it needed to be, and I took a big swing of the ax handle and hit that ball as hard as I could.

But as the baseball connected with that ax handle, the handle split and a big splinter went into the skin of my hand and began hurting like crazy.

Billy went to catch the pop-up, but when it came down, it went through Billy's hands and hit him in the nose.

So there both of us was laying on the ground in pain. Billy's nose was bleeding and my hand had a big splinter in it.

There's one thing that me and Billy sure learned today: Baseball can kill you!

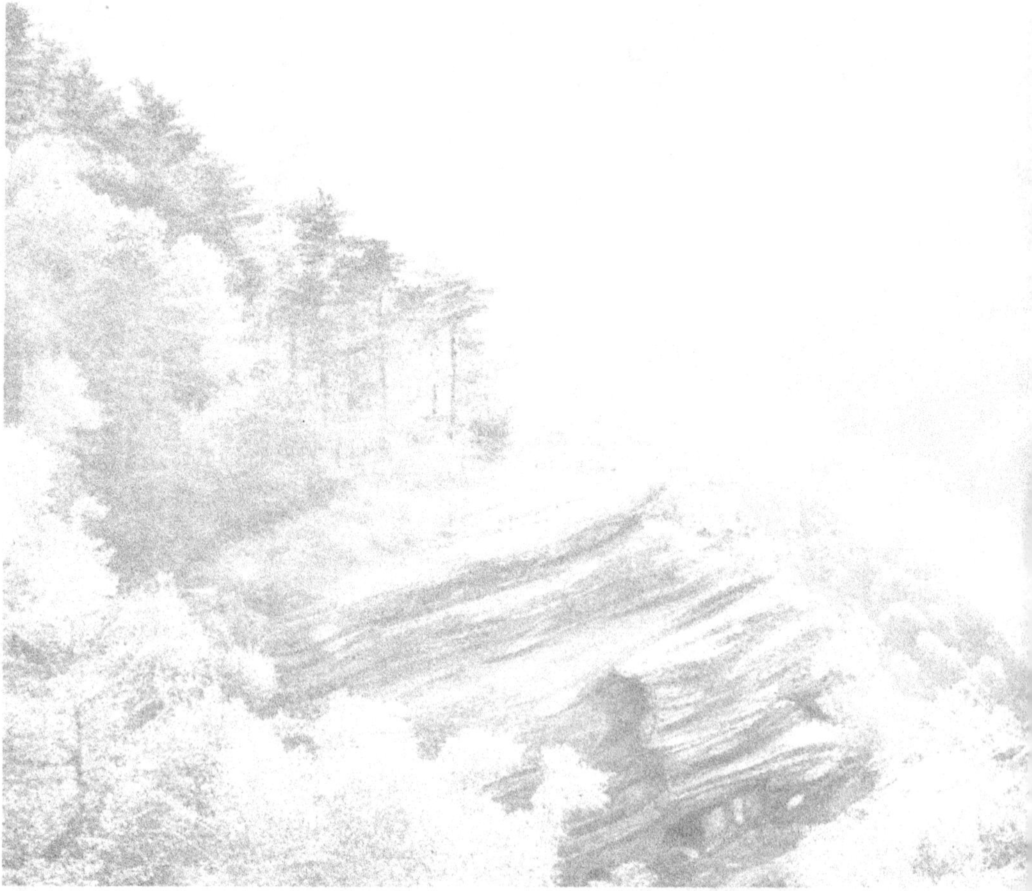

CHAPTER TWENTY-ONE

MR. NED

It was about the middle of the day, and me and Billy was sitting on the front porch trying to recover from our baseball adventures. That's when Mr. Ned pulled up in his truck filled with vegetables.

Mr. Ned is a farmer from up the road a spell, and he makes his living selling vegetables and the like. I believe he is sweet on Mommy, but I'm not for sure.

Mr. Ned came over to where me and Billy was sitting, and I had some ice on my lip and Billy had a wet washcloth on his nose, and Mr. Ned wanted to know if we'd been fighting.

"We were playing baseball and the baseball won," I replied.

I showed him the baseball and told him how me and Billy found it down at the river, and he thought it was a pretty nice baseball. Then he wanted to know where my mommy was, so I went in the house to get her.

I found Mommy in the kitchen looking at her reflection in the window trying to fix her hair. I asked her what she was doing and she told me none of my business. That's when I told her that Mr. Ned was outside and he wanted to talk to her, and she acted like she didn't even know Mr. Ned was around, but I think she knew the whole time.

Mommy went out to where Mr. Ned was and they sort of said howdy to each other and then they was quiet for a long time.

Suzie and Sally came outside and sat on the porch, and then Mary and Junior came walking around the house holding hands. Mr. Ned said it looked like we had a small army hanging around the house today, and I told him that it was just the usual army.

Mr. Ned said, "I've got some green tomatoes on the truck if you all want some."

"Why, Mr. Ned," Mommy said. "That's very neighborly of you, but we don't have any money to buy any green tomatoes."

"No charge," he said.

Well, that's all I needed to hear, and me and Sally ran over to the truck to get 'em. We could eat a whole truckload of fried green tomatoes if Mommy would let us.

Mr. Ned came over and got out a basket of that green gold from his truck and took 'em up to the porch and sat 'em down. I'm telling you, if we can get Mommy to fry us up some chicken with these tomatoes and some buttermilk biscuits, we'd be living fat all week.

Me and Billy toted that basket into the kitchen so Mommy could start frying them things right then and there. Sally and Suzie came in where we was and we all just surrounded that basket of green tomatoes as if we was looking at some sort of wonderful art of some kind.

That's when Suzie noticed that me and Billy was a bit rough looking.

"What on earth happened to the two of you?" she asked.

"We was playing baseball and things got out of hand," Billy said.

"You all look like you got beat up by a bunch of bullies," Sally said.

"Well, we still had fun," Billy told her.

That's when Sally said, "You all must not be too tough if you can be beat up by a baseball."

"It was our first day of baseballing," I said. "You can't get it right on the first day, right Billy?"

"That's right," he said. Then he told her that it was like playing the piano. "On the first day you're just trying to figure things out, and on the next day you're a little more at ease and things get a lot easier to do."

I think he's right about that. At least I hope he's right about it because I can't take too many more days of trying to figure out baseball or it just might kill me.

About that time Mary came into the kitchen because Junior had left to go back home.

I asked her, "Are you and Junior dating again?"

"I'm still thinking about it," she said.

Then Mary began looking around and started whispering to us.

"Do you know what I think? I think Mr. Ned is outside trying to get Mommy to go on a date."

"What makes you think that?" Sally asked.

"The signs."

"Signs? What are you talking about signs?" Suzie wanted to know.

"It's in their eyes."

"What about their eyes?" Billy asked.

"You can tell when two people are in love by the way they stare at each other."

Well, I wasn't one for signs. So I just went outside to where Mommy and Mr. Ned was standing and just asked 'em.

"Mr. Ned, are you asking my mommy out on a date?"

They stared at me like I had horns coming out of my head. Mommy turned all kinds of red and told me to get back in the house right now or there'd be a butt glowing in the house tonight.

So I went back inside not fully understanding what she got so mad about for. I mean, Mr. Ned is a nice fella and all. If she wants to date him, then go ahead and date him. Shoot fire, go on and marry him, I'd be all for it.

Imagine that, me having a stepdaddy that grows green tomatoes. Why, you can't beat that with a stick.

Eventually Mr. Ned left to get his vegetables to the market before they got all dried out standing in the sun. But he is coming over to our house tomorrow evening for supper.

The one downside to that was that Mommy decided to wait until then to fry up them green tomatoes, which made me and Sally pretty disappointed, but it gives us something to look forward to. Well, that's what Mommy said anyway.

As night came on and we all got ready for bed, I decided I was going to sleep with my baseball. After all, I had done and got all of mine and Billy's blood off of it, so it was clean for sleeping with. Tomorrow Billy is going to take it home and sleep with it. I guess it's kind of dumb to sleep with a baseball, but I don't care.

I told Mommy and my sissies that I was going to sleep with it and they laughed, but they just don't understand because they are all girls. Boys only understand about stuff like this.

I guess I'll go on to bed now. Let me get that baseball.

CHAPTER
TWENTY-TWO

LIGHTNING MAN

This morning I headed out to Billy's to take him the baseball so he could sleep with it tonight. As I was walking along the road, I seen a family of raccoons up in front of me about thirty feet. I stopped in my tracks and watched 'em. They was as cute as they could be. It looked like a momma and two babies. I must have stood there for about ten minutes and watched them before they went up into the woods. You just never know what you'll run into walking up or down this road.

I got to Billy's house and seen him hoeing in the garden. I went over to him and told him about them raccoons and he said that he hoped them raccoons was having a better time than he was because he's done and had about all of this day as he could handle. Poor ol' Billy had been hoeing corn all morning long.

"Well, you can cheer up, Billy, because I have done and brought you the baseball to sleep with tonight."

"I thank you, Price, but I don't even know if that's going to cheer me up or not," he said.

"Sure it will."

"You know what I think?"

"What's that?"

"There's way too much corn in the world."

With that, I decided to help him do his hoeing so maybe he could get done a lot quicker and then we could do something that was fun. I placed the baseball on a rock and got another hoe and went after them weeds like they was the enemy to fun. Which they was.

As we was hoeing, Billy said, "I've been doing me some thinking."

"About what?" I asked.

"I think me and you should come up with our own superhero and send it to them comic book companies and see if we could get rich."

Well, I didn't have to think about that too much to know that it sounded like a great idea.

"I like the way you think, Billy."

When I said that he stopped and just stared at me.

"You're the first person that has ever said that to me in my life," he said.

I thought the fella was going to cry right there in the corn, so I changed the subject back to superheroes.

"What should the hero be like?" I said.

"I've been trying to think about one as I hoed, but all I came up with was a boy that got ate by stalks of corn," Billy said.

"You've got corn on the brain. We need a name that would make every bad guy in the world shake in fear."

"How about Bird Man?"

"You're not even trying, Billy. They ain't nothing intimidating about a superhero called Bird Man. In fact, it's kind of silly."

"How about Frog?"

I just shook my head at that one. "Billy, you ain't even getting close to a good name."

"My granddaddy told me of a beast that was half frog and half man that lived on High Knob Mountain, and when you walked by him, he would jump out and wet all over you and then you get warts and go crazy."

I just stared at Billy after he told me that, knowing for sure that he has just uttered the stupidest thing I had ever heard tell of in my life.

"You're granddaddy was just pulling your leg," I said. "There ain't no such thing as a Frog Man in real life, and if I have anything to say about it, there won't be one in the comic books either."

"I believe it's true," said Billy.

"You're going to have to stop believing everything someone tells you or you're going to end up in a bunch of messes which you can't get out of when you get bigger."

"But it being true would be a good angle to sell our character. We could say it was real. That would get people excited and they'll want to read about it and we'll become rich."

"I ain't coming up with a superhero whose power is wetting all over people. He'd be kicked out of every superhero club in the world!"

"Well," Billy said, "I'd be scared of anyone that tried to pee all over me."

"We have to come up with a better name than Frog. A better name than Batman even, and that's going to take some serious thinking."

We hoed us some more and then Billy said, "Lightning Man."

"Lightning Man?"

"Yeah, we could say he was struck by lightning while hoeing corn and that gave him some sort of superpowers."

"I like the way your thinking has recovered from the frog thing, Billy. Well, except for the hoeing part. We might need to change that."

"Change it to what?"

"How about he was trying to rescue someone in a storm and the lightning struck him and then a few weeks later he realized he was different in some way."

"He could shoot lightning from his fists - that would scare any bad guy."

"I like that. We may be on the path of creating the greatest superhero that has ever been created by two boys hoeing corn."

"Would his pee be electric, too?"

"Stop it, Billy. We're not going to go there."

"I was just wondering-"

"You've got corn on the brain and now your granddaddy has done and given you pee on the brain, too."

"What if he shakes hands with you? Would you die? You know, by being electrocuted to death."

"Maybe he can control it somehow."

"He could wear special gloves."

"But if he had to wear special gloves, then people would know he was Lightning Man when he was in his secret identity."

"Clark Kent wears glasses and just takes them off to be Superman and no one notices."

"Gloves sort of stick out more than glasses, though, especially if it's in the summer. We'll just get to that part later."

We got to hoeing some more and then Billy's mommy came out and gave us something to drink and told us we could stop hoeing for the day and head on out to play. Me and Billy sat on that rock where I had put the baseball and kept talking about our superhero.

"We need some sort of superhero outfit for him. Maybe we could put lightning bolts on the side of his pants, and we could have a lightning bolt on his chest," I said.

"Yeah, and he could have a black cape and fly through the sky."

Billy then began running around the yard like he was flying. He started yelling that he was the Lightning Man and he was going to protect all of Wise County from evil.

I told Billy to come back over here and sit down until we can get all our ideas straight. So Billy sat back down and asked, "Who's going to draw it?"

Well, I was stumped. I didn't know of anybody that could draw as good as those artists could in the comic books. I told Billy that I could write the story, but I couldn't draw it. Billy said that maybe he could try and draw it by tracing some of them drawings out of the comic books and add some changes to it like the lightning bolts on the pants and such, and we could call it a rough sketch so that the comic book company would have a good idea of what our hero looked like.

I told him that might just work. In fact, I was pretty sure that it would work because anybody can trace something. How hard can that be?

But we still needed a bad guy. You can't have a hero without a bad guy because then there'd be no reason for a hero. Billy came up with the name Mr. Q, and I kind of liked it. We made Mr. Q a man that wore dark glasses and he could see in the dark. He couldn't fly, but he did have the desire to rule the world, which from what I read in the comic books was a requirement of all bad guys.

Now we had a story! Mr. Q wanted to rule the world and Lightning Man wouldn't let him. Then me and Billy went inside his house and had us a sandwich.

I couldn't stay too much longer at Billy's because Mr. Ned was coming over for supper, and Mommy told me that we all had to take us a shower before he came and put on our best clothes.

I thought that was a bit on the strange side, because I've never heard of having to take a shower to eat, being that we was going to be wearing clothes anyhow. But I'd do just about anything to eat me some of those fried green tomatoes, so shower here I come!

CHAPTER TWENTY-THREE

SUPPER WITH MR. NED

I stayed out on the front porch for some two hours waiting for Mr. Ned to come and eat supper with us. I have to say, I was more dolled up than I have ever been in my life. Shower, clean clothes, shoes and socks that match, and I didn't even leave the house.

Of course, I wasn't the only one all dressed up. Mommy had changed dresses five times, and she had put one of them on twice. She was more nervous than I had ever seen her before. Mary tried to keep her calm, but it wasn't really taking hold any.

I must confess that I thought I might just starve to death before he got here, but he did finally come. He was all gussied up with his hair slicked down and parted in the middle, and he was wearing a suit with work boots. He apologized to Mommy for wearing his work boots, but he said that was all he had and Mommy didn't seem to mind any.

It was a little strange to be out on a date with your mommy. I know that technically this wasn't called a date by the two main participants, but it was a date, and me and my sissies knew it.

During supper, Mr. Ned told us that he needed some help on the farm toting all his garden stuff back and forth from the store and to the side of the road where he does some selling to people that go by, and when he said that, I hit on an idea.

"Me and Billy could help do that for you Mr. Ned," I told him.

"You're a little young to be working, aren't you?"

"Apparently Billy ain't too young because his mommy pert near works him to death hoeing in the garden."

Everybody laughed and then Mr. Ned asked Mommy if it would be okay and she said it would be. Then Mary said that Junior could help out, too, and Mr. Ned thought that was a good idea.

"What are you going to charge to work for me?" he asked.

"I don't really know, but I sure could use me some money."

"What for?"

"I need it for some paper and pencils, and I have to buy me some stamps so me and Billy can send off our comic book idea to one of them comic book companies so that we can become rich."

Well, let me tell you, everybody at the table was all for me and Billy getting rich, so Mr. Ned welcomed me aboard and told me to bring Billy and Junior to work first thing in the morning, and I told him I would make sure they got there on time.

We finished eating our crawdads and fried green tomatoes, and Mary made me, Suzie, and Sally come into the kitchen and wash the dishes while Mommy and Mr. Ned talked in the piano room. I was not too happy about this. Washing dishes was women work, and that's what I told Mary. That's when she hit me in the back of the head with her hand and said, "Well, get to it, woman."

Sally laughed and told me right to my face that tonight I was a woman.

So there I was washing them dishes feeling like I was lower than the contents of a snake's belly. I sure hope Lightning Man doesn't find out about this.

What I should have done was made the bad guy in my comic book a woman. Just an everyday big-mouth woman, just like all of my sissies! But I wanted my fellow to win every now and then. Something a boy with three sissies never gets to do.

CHAPTER
TWENTY-FOUR

FIRST DAY OF WORK

I got up and headed over to Billy's and found him outside on his front porch looking at Batman comic books. I told him I got us a job helping Mr. Ned and he couldn't believe it.

I said, "Go kiss your mommy and tell her we're going to work. Not just kid work, either. This is paying work."

Billy got all excited. He couldn't believe we were going to be paid just like men. He went and told his mommy, and she wasn't too sure about it at first, and then I told her what we'd be doing and she knew Mr. Ned pretty good so she said it was okay. Billy's daddy was already gone to work in the coal mines, so he was excited to be able to tell him this evening that he's got a job.

Billy's mommy wanted to know if we were going to be working by ourselves, and I told her that Junior was going to be helping and that Mary had headed out earlier this morning to tell him that she got him a job.

She then asked if she should pack us a lunch and I told her that I didn't rightly know for sure. Billy said if we was toting garden stuff we could probably just take us a bite of that, and I told him you can't eat what Mr. Ned is trying to sell or he'd take it out of our pay and we needed all the pay we could get.

So Billy's mommy made us a sandwich each and put 'em in a bag and set 'em on the porch for us to take with us.

During that time, Billy showed me his tracing of Batman, which he changed some to look like Lightning Man. It didn't look too good. I thought anyone could trace, but I guess I was wrong. However, we didn't have time to go over it too much because we had to get to work.

On our way, Junior came up behind us in his daddy's truck, and he wanted to know if we wanted us a ride over to Mr. Ned's, and we both said yes and we got in the back of Junior's truck and he drove us over there.

We got there and we seen Mr. Ned going in his chicken house, and we all three made our way inside. When we walked in, I was a bit overwhelmed with what I was seeing. That chicken house had more chickens in it than I had ever seen in my life. There was more chickens in there than raindrops in a storm. I swear the sound of them chickens could make your ears hurt.

Mr. Ned seen us and he said we could go to the back porch and start loading the vegetables and eggs into the truck. He had already put everything on the porch waiting for us. At least that's what we thought he said, as it was kind of hard to tell exactly because of all those chickens clucking at the same time.

So we all three headed out of the chicken house and over to the porch when Billy thought we should have a bad guy in our comic book that was part chicken. Junior started to laugh and wanted to know what we were talking about and I told him about our Lightning Man idea.

He didn't seem too impressed, and I asked him did he have a better idea. He didn't. Some people just like to criticize other peoples' achievements, I reckon.

We started loading up the truck, and after about half an hour we were done. Mr. Ned came over and said we did good and then we all piled up in the cab of his truck and took off to his favorite selling place.

I tell you what's the truth, that is the most uncomfortable I've ever been in my life, riding inside that truck with three other fellows. Junior was sitting near the door and I was in Junior's lap. Billy was sitting in the middle at the gear shift, and he was being squeezed by everybody.

There was a book on the dashboard and I looked through it and halfway in it was a map. I had never seen a book of words that had a map in the middle of it. I've seen road maps before, but I didn't know they put maps in word books. My first day on the job and I'm expanding my learning already - and it ain't even noon yet.

We finally made it to a wide place in the road, which was about twenty feet or so in size, with woods on the back edge of it. It had pretty good traffic flow along the road for potential customers. (I'm telling you the size in case someday somebody reading this wants to make them a map of what I'm telling them.) As we got out we set up something like a tent in the back of the truck which gave us plenty of shade during the hot day. As we were fixing everything up, some people already pulled over to see what Mr. Ned had for sale.

That's when I seen Billy hit his leg with his fist. He seemed pretty upset.

"What's the matter, Billy?" I asked.

"I left them sandwiches that Mommy made for us on the porch. Now we don't have anything to eat."

"I wouldn't worry about it none," I told him. "If we need to we'll go in the woods and see if we can find us something."

"What are we going to eat in the woods?"

"I don't know. I'm sure there's something."

"I ain't eating no worms or anything like that."

"I never said we were."

"I don't want worm breath. Girls don't like that."

"What do you care about what girls think of worm breath?"

"I care."

About that time, a big car pulled up and a man wearing a suit got out and started to look at Mr. Ned's stuff. Junior said hello to him and asked if he needed him some string beans. The man wanted to know who owned all of this, and we pointed to Mr. Ned, and the man went over to him and they began talking.

It looked like important talk to me, but I wasn't really sure being that it was just my first day of man work.

It turned out that man was from Roanoke and he owned him a chain of grocery stores throughout the south and he wanted to buy all of Mr. Ned's stuff and any more he might have back at his farm.

When that man left, Mr. Ned came over and told us, and then he showed us this big wad of money which that man gave him. He said that he was going to send some trucks out to Mr. Ned's house and fill 'em up with vegetables and eggs and such because his regular supplier was having problems meeting his needs. Then Mr. Ned gave me and Billy and Junior a whole dollar for helping him, and we didn't even work two hours.

He told us that we were his good luck charm.

Well, the three of us looked at our dollars and we didn't know what to do. Billy began dancing around saying he was rich, and I guess for once anyway, we truly was.

We spent the rest of the day watching and helping a little as a bunch of men came from that store fella and loaded up the trucks with Mr. Ned's vegetables. What little we helped wasn't too hard, though me and Billy wasn't strong enough to lift some of it, but we pitched in our share just fine.

I got back to the house and I ran inside and showed everybody my dollar. They couldn't believe their eyes, and to tell you the truth, I was having problems believing it, too.

A whole dollar. I could get me a writing tablet and go see me one of them moving pictures down at the Movie Palace. I hope they're showing a cowboy picture. That would be fantastic! Or maybe even a superhero picture.

Then when I got finished watching my movie, I'd head on over to the store and get my writing tablet and start on my Lightning Man comic book. This was the best of days.

But then I got to thinking. Here I have a whole dollar, and Mommy could use it to buy some things around the house. So I gave it to her. I thought I should try and help the family out instead of spending the money on myself.

Mary was giving piano lessons to help the family and Sally and Suzie was always sewing to help, too, so I guess I felt a little guilty about not helping pay the bills.

As I went to bed, I thought a lot about it. I really think I did the right thing. I was proving myself, like a man should.

Mommy told me I didn't have to do that, but I knew I did.

I do still wonder what was playing down at the Movie Palace, though.

CHAPTER
TWENTY-FIVE

SALLY'S IN LOVE

Me and Sally headed on out to the river with our fishing poles and our can of worms this morning, and I have to say it got curiouser and curiouser as we went, because from the moment we got on our way, she got to talking about Billy. In fact, I'd say that was all she wanted to talk about.

"Do you think Billy's cute?" Sally asked.

"What kind of crazy question is that to ask a fella?" I asked her in my hollering voice, and it was the right voice to use, too.

"I was just wondering what you thought."

"I don't think about it at all," I told her.

"He seems strong."

"Well, I guess he's as strong as could be expected for his age."

"I was talking with Suzie, and she told me that she wasn't interested in Billy none, so I've decided to take him."

I couldn't help but ask, "Are we talking about the same Billy?"

"Yep."

"Does Billy get a say in this?"

"Nope."

We got to our fishing rock, but Sally kept talking about Billy. She seemed right obsessed with him.

"What in tarnation has got you so interested in Billy?" I asked.

She said, "Mary will probably be marrying up with Junior one day, and that got me to thinking that I should plan up."

"Plan up?"

"Yeah, pick me a fella now so I don't have to worry about it later."

"So you're trying to get your husband out of the way now."

"Exactly."

We fished us a spell, and then she asked me, "Do you think Billy likes me?"

"Does it matter?" I asked.

"It might."

"Billy seems to like all girls both living and dead, so I'd think that would cover you."

"Well, when he's officially my beau, he'll have to stop liking girls right then and there."

"I think that will happen real fast after he becomes your beau," I told her.

"Do you think I'm pretty?"

"No brother thinks their sister is pretty."

"Just answer my question. I'm not going to tell anybody."

"I guess. … Can't we talk about something else?"

"When you see Billy again, you tell him that I like him and see if that's okay with him or not."

"I'll do it. But why don't you tell him when he comes over for piano practice?"

"Ladies don't do things like that. We're too delicate."

That's when she stuck the hook through a worm and cast it out toward the log that was in the middle of the river.

Poor Billy.

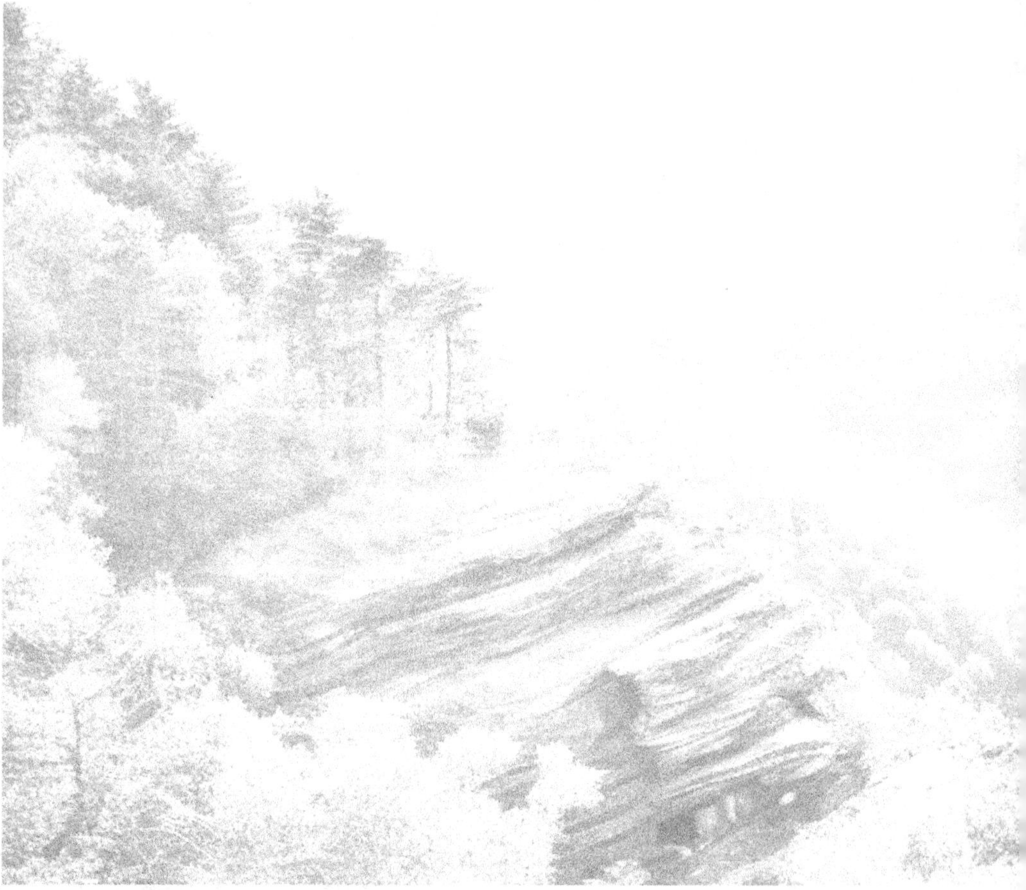

CHAPTER
TWENTY-SIX

FRANKENSTEIN

Around one o'clock, I went into town for Mommy. I had to get her some thread and take some clothes that she sewed to the store to see if they might sell. It was women's clothes, and I hated having to carry 'em around. I was of the mind that girls should carry girls clothes and boys should carry boys clothes and then the world would be just fine, but being I'm outnumbered by girls at my house, this boy had to tote girls clothes.

So there I was walking down the road carrying a bunch of women's clothes in the middle of the day. I was sure hoping no one I knew would see me. If Batman found out, he wouldn't let me read him anymore for sure.

I had told Mommy to let one of my sissies take 'em into town, but she said she had them doing something else so it was up to me and to stop talking about it and get going.

I got into town and went into the store and laid them clothes down on the counter, and I sure was happy to get rid of them. Junior was there, and he took the clothes and put 'em in a box in the back for his daddy to look over and price. I got the thread and paid for it with the money that Mommy gave me, and Junior wanted to know if I was going to get something with my dollar that Mr. Ned gave me.

"I gave it to Mommy," I told him.

"All of it?"

"Yeah."

"Why?"

"I thought she could use it to pay some bills and such."

He looked at me and said, "You're a good man, Price Mullins. Not many kids your age would do something like that."

I have to admit that I felt pretty proud when he told me that.

"What are you going to do with your dollar?" I asked him.

"I'm going to the Movie Palace for the two o'clock show. *Frankenstein's* playing."

"What's that about?"

"It's about a man that makes a monster. It's supposed to be real scary. Do you want to go?"

"I don't got no money," I told him.

"I'll buy you a ticket since I still have my dollar."

Well, I didn't have to think twice about that and told him let's get going.

"Now, it's scary," Junior told me. "Are you sure you want to go see it?"

"I just carried a bunch of girls clothes into town, so I'm not scared of no movie," I said.

So two o'clock rolled around, and there me and Junior was standing in line to see a monster movie. My very first movie! This was one of the most exciting days of my life.

When we went up to the ticket window, I seen the poster for *Frankenstein,* and I have to confess that I swallowed pretty hard as I seen that thing's face.

"Do you still want to go in?" Junior asked.

"I'm going in. No monster is going to keep me from seeing my first movie."

So we went in and gave this man our ticket, and he tore it in half and gave me one end of it. I didn't know what I was supposed to do with it, but Junior told me to keep it in my pocket so in case I had to leave the movie I could get back in by showing them my ticket stub, and I wouldn't have to pay again to get in.

"There's no way I would leave before the movie was over. That's just dumb," I told him.

"We'll see," he said.

We went in and sat down, and Junior said he'd be right back. I didn't really know what I was supposed to do. When he came back, he had some popcorn and some pop.

"Where'd you get that?"

"They sell it in the lobby."

I couldn't believe this. Now, I've had popcorn before, but I've never had a pop. I once found an old bottle of pop on the ground with some still in it and took a drink of it, but it tasted terrible. However, that might not have been a good test.

It was called Coca-Cola, and it was fantastic. Mommy always told me that it would rot my teeth out, but she says that about eating raw potatoes, too.

That movie started right after they turned out all of the lights. At first I thought we had a power failure and I wasn't going to get to see my movie, but Junior said they always play the movie in the dark. I guess they do that to make you more scared.

I'd like to write something about the movie in my diary here, but I was so scared that I found myself looking at the floor most of the time. Junior didn't seem scared at all, but I sure was.

I do remember that one man on the big screen shouted, "It's alive! It's alive!" I have to say that gave me the creeps. I did see the monster's face, and I think my eyes must have got bigger than silver dollars when I seen him. But I didn't leave. I stayed there and watched it. Well, I watched most of it, but it still counts as staying.

There was some screaming by the other people watching, but I can say proudly I wasn't one of them. I didn't put my hands over my face, either. My tactic was to look down at the floor when I got scared. Maybe that's why they turned the lights off - so nobody knew who was screaming and looking away.

But even though I was scared the whole time I really did enjoy myself. I got to see a movie and I had a Coca-Cola, after all. It was truly a big day for Price Mullins.

I got to the house around five o'clock, and Mommy wasn't too happy as she met me on the front porch.

"Where have you been?"

"Mommy, I just had the best day of my life."

I gave her the thread that she had me go get and she stared at me real curious like.

"You didn't steal anything, did you?"

I have no idea why that entered her mind for. I just told her that Junior took me to see a movie down at the Movie Palace.

"You watched a movie? What kind of movie?"

"It was a monster movie."

I really believe if she was a bag of corn she would have popped right there.

"I don't like that one bit," she told me.

"It wasn't a bad movie. It was just scary, is all."

And I have to say that the scary feeling was repeating itself at that very moment.

"I think I need to have a word with Junior," Mommy said.

"Well, don't yell at him. He was just being nice."

"Nice? You'll have nightmares tonight, and I'll be the one that has to deal with it."

"I'm not going to have any nightmares."

"Why would he take you to a movie anyways?"

"I told him that I gave my dollar to you to help pay the bills and he said he'd take me to the movies."

She didn't say anything to that. She just stared at me and looked down at the ground and then turned and went back into the house.

I don't know what that means exactly, but I think it might mean that Junior won't get into any trouble. Well, with Mommy, that is.

Later I was getting ready to go to sleep when Mary came in my bedroom. She sat down on the edge of my bed.

"I think it was nice of you to give your dollar to Mommy."

I just nodded.

"Did Billy get a dollar, too?"

"He sure did. Me, Billy and Junior all got dollars from Mr. Ned."

"Junior got a dollar?"

"Yeah."

Mary then had a smile begin to form on her face.

"Did Junior say what he was going to do with his dollar?"

At this point I was starting to get a little scared on behalf of Junior.

"Why?"

"I was just thinking that a fellow might want to get his girl a present. I thought maybe you might know what it was he was getting me."

Oh, boy. I knew that Junior was in big-time trouble now because he spent it all on me and him going to the movies.

"I'm sure he'll get you something nice," I said as I tried to think of some way to protect my new buddy.

"How nice?"

"I sure am sleepy," I made on like.

"You can tell me, I won't tell Junior you told me."

I didn't know what to do. I got to feeling like that monster surrounded by them people with fire torches. Any move I made could get me killed.

"I think it would be best if I left any present giving to Junior."

She seemed to think that meant that he got her something good, and she left my room as happy as she could be.

I had to warn Junior, but I didn't know how exactly. But I knew I had to because a life was at stake.

Oh, and Mommy was right - I did have nightmares about that monster. But I didn't tell anybody.

CHAPTER TWENTY-SEVEN

THE GOAT AND LOVER BILLY

I heard Mary say this morning that Junior was coming over, so I decided to wait out on the front porch for him so I could warn him that Mary was expecting him to get her a present with that dollar he got.

As I was sitting there doing my waiting, I thought I had heard me something walking around in the woods. I didn't pay it no mind at first, thinking it was just birds or squirrels or something like that. They can make some pretty big noises even though they're just little fellows.

But that noise kept on and I started to get curious, not to mention bored waiting for Junior to come. So I decided to head on into the woods and see what was making all of that commotion.

I walked up there as careful as I could because I got to thinking it might be something bigger than I was thinking it was. My mind started thinking about that monster movie I saw yesterday, and that wasn't no help at all.

The farther I went up into the woods, the scareder I got. What if it was that bear that came upon our porch awhile back? What in the world would I do if I faced a bear? Well, I'm pretty sure I'd die, but hopefully I'd try and defend myself somehow. So I decided I better pick me up a rock to throw in case it was something that needed a rock thrown at it.

The noise got louder and louder until I almost couldn't take it, and then I seen it. It was a goat.

Someone's goat has got out of its fence and has made its way over here. So I started talking to it and asked it what it was doing up here in the woods. I don't know why I started talking to it because I know goats can't talk, but my only other alternative was to throw my rock at it, and I didn't think I needed to do that.

But I must have said the right thing, because that goat came right over to where I was and started nuzzling me with its nose. Then he took its front feet and jumped up and sat 'em on my chest just like a dog would when he wanted you to pet it.

So I started petting it and it seemed to like it. As I was petting it, I looked down at the road and watched Junior drive up. I couldn't believe my bad luck - or his, for that matter - because I needed to warn him about Mary and I was about as far away from him as I could get.

So I pushed the goat away and headed through the woods as fast as I could. Well, it wasn't long before I tripped and fell over a log and rolled down that hill and ended up in a muddy ditch.

I tell you what, when I hit that ditch it knocked the breath clean out of me. I kept trying to breathe, but nothing was happening. Finally the air came back into my lungs and I was able to get back up.

I started running up the road when I noticed that goat was chasing me. When it caught up, it kept biting me on the seat of my pants, and it smarted like crazy.

I stopped and turned to that goat and shouted, "You need to get on outta here because I'm on a rescue mission. Now get!"

I started running again, and that goat began chasing after me and got all tangled up in my feet and I fell smack dab into a mud hole.

I got up and looked at my hands all scratched up and bleeding, and then that goat jumped back on my chest with its front feet wanting me to pet it some more.

I knew at that moment that goat didn't escape from its pen. It had been turned loose by its owner because it ain't nothing but bad luck.

I got that goat off of my chest and got to running again with that goat hot on my heels. I seen Junior get out of his truck, and I started shouting for him not to go inside the house, but he didn't hear me and I watched him go on the front porch and knock on the door.

I got to the driveway and I had to stop and rest, and that's when I seen Junior go into the house. I was too late, and I have to admit, a little tired from the running and fighting a goat. Now I had to come to terms with the fact that Junior's going to be dead by sunset and it was all my fault.

That's when I looked over at the wood house and seen Billy talking to Suzie. That goat was still nipping at me when I saw Billy giving Suzie a present, so me and that goat went over there to where they was at to see what was going on.

"What are you doing, Billy?"

"Talking to Suzie."

He whispered into my ear, "I got her a present with my dollar."

This wasn't good at all, because I now have two love murders on my hands with Junior inside the house with Mary, and now Sally was going to kill Billy.

"Where did you get that goat?" Suzie asked.

"I found it in the woods. Uh, Suzie, can I talk to you for a second?"

Suzie came over to me and I tried to explain some things to her.

"I thought you didn't like Billy."

"I don't."

"Then why are you taking that present from him then?"

"It's the Christian thing to do."

"It's not Christian to take a present from a fellow that you don't like when he's giving you the present because he wants you to be his girl when Sally is inside wanting him to be her beau and he don't know anything about her liking him."

"I'll tell him all of them details later."

"Later? Why not now?"

"Because I haven't opened the present up yet, dummy. I want to see what it is."

Just then Billy let out a scream. I turned to where he was, and that goat had done and pinned poor ol' Billy down onto the ground.

"Get this goat off of me before it eats me!" Billy shouted.

Now, if my life wasn't already complicated enough, I looked over to my right and here came Sally. She seen that present in Suzie's hands and then seen Billy pinned beneath that goat, and I reckon she knew what had happened. Well, I doubt she knew why there was a goat on Billy for, but I'm pretty sure she knew that Billy had given a present to the wrong Mullins.

"Suzie Mullins, what are you doing with my man?" Sally shouted.

"I'm not doing anything with your man," said Suzie.

"That present was meant for me!" shouted Sally.

"Apparently not!" shouted Suzie.

Billy started crying, as that goat wouldn't get off of him, and then before I knew it, Suzie and Sally was fighting and I ran to get Mommy.

I got up to the porch when I ran into Junior running out of the house yelling for his life.

He was saying, "Sunflower, I love you and I didn't spend that dollar on another girl!" And that's when Mary came out with a broom and was brooming him but good.

I got inside and found Mommy and told her, "Hurry up, Suzie and Sally are fighting!"

So Mommy grabbed the fly swatter and we both headed out the door as fast as we could.

Mommy got over to Sally and Suzie and began swatting them on the legs with that fly swatter, and they stopped fighting and grabbed their legs begging Mommy to stop whipping them.

Then once that got settled, Mommy asked them what they was fighting about and where in the world did that goat come from.

"Suzie stole my present," Sally said.

"I didn't steal anything. Billy gave it to me," Suzie said back.

"He meant to give it to me!" shouted Sally.

"Why?" asked Mommy.

"Because I love him!" Sally screamed.

Everything suddenly stopped. Even the goat.

Sally became embarrassed and took off into the house.

"Suzie," Mommy said, "you get in the house, too. I'm not going to let my daughters fight like cats and dogs."

Suzie took off inside with her present and Mommy looked at Billy.

"Is that your goat?"

"No, ma'am," said Billy. Then he begged her not to hit him with the fly swatter because he bruised easily. She said she wasn't going to swat him with it, then she asked again about the goat.

"It followed me from out of the woods," I said.

"Well, you take it back where you found it."

"But it won't stay where I found it."

"Do as I tell you or I'll use the fly swatter on you."

Then Mommy headed into the house and I went over to Billy.

"Are you okay?"

"I'll be fine if you keep your goat away from me."

"It ain't my goat."

"I bet its name is Devil."

"That wouldn't surprise me none," I told him.

"Why were your sissies fighting for?"

"They was fighting over you," I told him.

"Me?" he asked in a high-pitched voice, and the expression that came over his face would make you think that I had told him that he just won first prize in a pig-calling contest.

"I never had girls fight over me before."

"You best get used to it, because I'm sure they'll be at it again."

"Who won?"

"The fly swatter."

"What?"

"Mommy broke it up before either could win. Didn't you pay any attention to this?"

"I couldn't hear because of all of my screaming because of that goat. All I knew was that Sally and Suzie was fighting, but I didn't know why."

"Did you hear what Sally said?"

"I thought she said she loved me, but I figured I heard wrong."

"You heard right."

Billy thought about it some and said, "Just my luck, I gave a present to the wrong girlfriend, and now they're fighting over me."

"You lead an interesting life."

"Why don't Suzie then just give the present to Sally and everything is fixed?"

"You don't know anything about girls, do you?"

"No. Just that I want one. I've not really thought about it any further beyond that point."

"Suzie will now like you for spite. It's the way sissies are. They don't want one to get ahead of 'em. So they'll be fighting over you for days now."

He thought about it a bit and then asked, "Do I go with the winner or the loser?"

You know something? I don't think Billy really cared which of my sissies got him just as long as one of them did.

I was done talking girls, so I said, "I have to take this goat back into the woods where I found him. Do you want to go?"

"Sure."

We headed off toward the woods, and that goat took turns at jumping on us. That's when I seen Junior and Mary over by the truck, and they appeared to be liking each other again, so I didn't see any reason for me to go over there and tell Mary about the movie.

As we walked, Billy said, "I have me two girlfriends now."

"You might not after today, so I wouldn't brag too loud."

"Thing is, I don't have enough money to get presents for two girlfriends."

"What was that present anyway?"

"Candy. All girls like candy."

"I suppose that's good to know."

We got to where I had found that goat earlier and told it to get to where it belongs. He just looked at us like we was crazy. We tried shooing him away, but it didn't do any good. It was like trying to talk to a, well, goat.

The goat then jumped on Billy and knocked him down, and he started screaming again for me to get it off. I couldn't help but laugh at him. What my sissies see in him I will never understand. Unless, of course, they want a man that was easy to beat up, and Billy is overqualified for that position.

I got the goat off Billy and took it up farther into the woods. It then went down over the hill, and I turned to Billy and told him let's get out of here before it comes back.

We took off running back to the house and then laid down beneath the tree to rest.

"I can't believe you spent a whole dollar on candy for a girl."

"I didn't. I bought a bunch of comic books, and with the money I had left over, I got the candy. I bought it for Mommy, but she didn't like it, so I thought I'd just give it to Suzie. You know, to show how devoted I am to her."

"I see. The problem with that is that you gave the candy to the wrong girl. Suzie doesn't like you, Sally does."

"Well, I don't have no more candy to give away. Do you think Sally likes comic books?"

When he said that, I laid down the law right then and there.

"You ain't giving my sissy any comic books. Them's mine!"

CHAPTER
TWENTY-EIGHT

BULLIES

Me and Billy went fishing this afternoon. We decided it might be best to leave my sissies alone while they figured out which one of them was going to get Billy. Though Billy did want to stay and watch 'em, I told him that he didn't want to be around two sissies fighting before they was done because you'd end up right in the middle of it and they could punch pretty hard.

We got to our spot and started fishing when I noticed two big boys standing up the road looking down at us. I didn't know who they were, but I was hoping they were nice.

"Hi," I said in an attempt to let them know that we were friendly, but they didn't say anything back.

At that point, I started to get a little worried.

Billy looked at them and waved, then asked right friendly like, "How you fellows doing?"

Again they didn't say anything.

Billy whispered, "Who are they?"

"I don't know."

"Why are they just standing there looking at us for?"

"I don't know."

"What do we do?"

"I don't know."

"You know, Price," Billy said. "Having you with me right now isn't really showing much of a payoff."

I guess I could see his point, but I truly didn't know what I was supposed to do. All I wanted them to do was leave.

However, they didn't.

In fact, they came down there where we was, and I started to get real scared. One of them just stared at me.

"What are you doing?" he asked me.

"Just fishing," I told him back.

"I don't remember you asking us for permission to fish our spot."

"I didn't know it was your spot."

I knew it decidedly *wasn't* their spot because I've fished here forever and never once did I ever see them here. But they was bigger than me and Billy, so I thought it might be best to just leave.

"Let's go, Billy."

We started to leave and one of them boys grabbed me by the arm.

"You can't leave here without me giving you permission to leave. Do you understand me?"

I felt as big as an ant at this point, but all I wanted to do was leave, so I just asked, "May I have your permission to leave?"

That's when he pushed me down and they both started laughing at me. I got to thinking what in the world have I got myself into now.

Billy helped me up.

"Looks like his girlfriend is worried about him."

"I'm not his girlfriend!" Billy shouted.

Then that boy got up in Billy's face and said, "Did you just yell at me?"

Billy didn't know what to do. I got up and said, "We're leaving. Come on, Billy."

"You two aren't going anywhere. You've been fishing our spot, so you have to be punished."

"We didn't know it was your spot," I said. "We're sorry and now we're leaving."

But they wouldn't let us leave. In fact they both began pushing me and Billy down onto the ground, and every time we got back up, they pushed us down again and laughed at us.

"Stop pushing us down!" I yelled.

"What are you going to do about it?" one of them asked.

I didn't do anything. I just stood there looking down at the ground. I was completely humiliated.

That's when the other bully picked Billy up and threw him into the river. Then they picked me up and threw me into the river.

Me and Billy stood there watching them boys laugh at us. Then they took our worm can and fishing poles and left with them.

Me and Billy started to cry. We didn't say anything to each other. All we did was cry, and then we both headed home. We just wanted out of there as fast as possible and to get this day over with.

I didn't know what I was going to tell Sally about her pole being stolen by them two bullies, but I'd worry about that later.

When I got home, Mommy wanted to know why I was all wet. I just told her that me and Billy was playing down at the river and fell in. I don't think she believed me, but I wasn't going to tell her the truth.

I went and took me a real cold shower and spent the rest of the day in my bedroom.

I hope Billy is okay. This is easily one of the worst days of my life, and no doubt he was feeling the same.

I couldn't sleep all night. All I could think about was them boys and wondering why I didn't try and fight 'em. Being beat up would feel a whole lot better than how I felt right now.

I know Mommy wouldn't have wanted me to fight, but sometimes you have to, just like my sissies did when they were fighting over Billy. I don't know if that's a good example or not, but it's the only one I could come up with.

In the middle of the night, I decided to get up and get me a drink of water. If we had beer I would have drunk that because that's how depressed I was feeling.

As I was going into the kitchen I heard something in there. I thought maybe them boys had come here to beat me up, so I thought to wake up Mommy, but then I stopped.

If they wanted me this bad, well, I'll give 'em what for. I'll not stand in the river crying anymore!

I went into the kitchen and turned the light on, and do you know what I saw? It was that goat! It had got in through the opened kitchen window and was knocking over everything in its path and emptying out all of the cabinets. It was a complete mess.

"You crazy goat! Get on out of here!" I shouted at it.

I went over to try and get it out of the kitchen, and it started bucking and kicking at me, so I went and got Mommy and she came into the kitchen and she just about lost it. If my mommy was ever going to cuss in her life, it was going to be right then.

"Get that goat out of here before I turn it into a stew!" Mommy screamed.

Now, I don't know how you get a goat out of a kitchen. In fact, I doubt anyone does. But I was given orders from Mommy on high, so I decided to just call him out.

"Come on goat, we're taking you outside."

So I walked to the door, and do you know that goat followed me right on out. It was like having a dog with horns.

I stood outside with it and said, "You've got to scat on out of here before my mommy cooks you."

I pushed him to try and get him to leave, but he wouldn't go. He just kept trying to jump on my chest so that I would pet him. Nothing is more depressing than having an animal that wants you to pet it when you ain't in a petting mood.

I finally picked me up some rocks and threw them at him to try and get him to go. I sure hated doing it because it made me feel sort of like being the bully. He just wanted to play, but all he was doing was getting on people's nerves.

He finally went off into the woods, and me and my sissies went into the kitchen to try and clean everything up.

I must admit that I think I lead the strangest life ever written down on paper.

CHAPTER TWENTY-NINE

COURAGE

I couldn't wait to get to my journal and tell what happened today.

This was the day that Billy was supposed to come for his piano practice. He had been coming just about every other day even though all he was supposed to come was once a week, but he liked playing the piano and he didn't have one at his house to bang on, so he would bring his nickel for his lesson and bang on our piano for an hour. And, of course, there was the fact that he liked hanging out with my sissies.

Well, I wasn't surprised that he didn't come today because he was probably still feeling the same way I was feeling about yesterday with them bullies throwing us into the river and stealing our fishing poles and that we didn't try and fight 'em none.

So I thought maybe it was best if I went over to Billy's so that maybe we could try and encourage each other. I was going to need his help to try and tell Sally what happened to her fishing pole, which was complicated by the fact that I didn't even ask for her permission to take it for Billy to use, so she doesn't even know it's missing yet.

As I was walking along, I heard something coming from the woods. I couldn't make it out at first, but the more I listened to it the more it sounded like someone yelling for help. So I tried tracking where them shouts were coming from. I walked up into the woods looking in all directions. I went through I don't know how many briars and such, but I thought someone must need some help, so I just kept going forward and tried to ignore all the scratches that I was getting.

The closer I got to the noise, I knew for sure it was someone crying for help. It sounded like two people now, so all kinds of thoughts were running through my head.

I thought it might be best if I was cautious about getting too close right off until I could figure out what was going on, so I got down on my belly and crawled to the top of a hill and looked over it through all these thorns, and there I flat seen it. It was them two boys that threw me and Billy into the river. They were up in a tree screaming for their lives. And do you know what was at the foot of that tree scaring them mean ol' boys to death? It was that goat!

I believe I smiled the biggest smile I had ever smiled in my life. I went down to that tree and looked at them boys and asked, "What are you two fellers doing in that tree?"

"That stupid goat attacked us!" one of 'em shouted.

"This goat?" I asked and almost laughed out loud but kept it inside me.

"Yes, that goat!" shouted back the other one.

"Do you not like being attacked by strangers?"

They didn't say anything. That's when I noticed mine and Sally's fishing poles at the base of the tree, and I picked 'em up.

"What are you going to do with our fishing poles?" one of them shouted.

"I'm taking them home with me where they belong, and if you don't like it, I'll get my goat to kill you two right here and now!"

That got 'em mad. Probably a little too mad, because one of them started down that tree for me, but the goat seen him coming down and started bucking and kicking and growling, and that boy climbed up even farther than he was before.

I told that goat to come on with me, and I petted it on its head and gave it a kiss right smack on the lips. I did! And what's more, I don't care who finds out about it either.

So me and that goat - the world's greatest goat, in my estimation - headed toward Billy's.

When I got there, his mommy told me that Billy was in his room, so I went around the side of the house to his window and looked in.

There was that poor ol' Billy sitting on his bed with his head down looking at the floor. I knew exactly how he felt, too.

"Hey, Billy."

"Hey," he told me back.

He was super depressed. That's when I lifted up the fishing poles for him to see, and his eyes brightened up immediately.

"How did you get 'em back?" he shouted as he ran over to the window. "Did you kill them boys? If you did, I won't tell. I'll even help you bury them. We got a shovel in the barn. Oh, man we could bury 'em in that bat poop under the bridge."

"I didn't kill 'em," I told him.

"Then who did?"

"Nobody killed anybody."

"Then how did you get the fishing poles back?"

That's when the goat put its front legs up on the window sill and I proudly announced, "This goat got 'em back for us."

"That goat?"

"He treed them boys in the woods, and they left the poles down on the ground, and I picked 'em up and brought 'em here for you to see."

"You're making all that up," he said.

"It's true. I wouldn't lie about that. In fact, it's too stupid to be true. But it is. Honest."

"He did all of that?"

"He sure did. Why, I think he would have eaten them fellows if I hadn't come along."

"Why do you reckon that goat likes us but hated them mean ol' boys?"

"Animals can tell good people from bad people. If they like you, they jump on your chest and try to get you to pet 'em. If they hate you, then you have to find a tree to get into, and you better find it fast."

Billy came out through the window so he could pet the world's greatest goat. He got down on his knees and hugged its neck. "Thank you Mr. Goat. You really made my day."

"I was so proud of that goat that I kissed it right on the mouth," I told him.

"Well, I'm going to do it, too."

So he gave that goat a big ol' smooch, and we played with that goat at Billy's pretty much all day.

At one point, Billy went into his house and got a hairbrush that his mommy never uses - well, I think she never uses it - for us to groom our goat with. Of course, if she knew what happened to us and what that goat did, then I don't think she would mind even if she does use it.

So we groomed that goat with that hairbrush for about an hour, and we sung to it and got it some water and picked some berries for it and pretty much spoiled that goat rotten. We enjoyed every minute of it.

"Shouldn't we name it?" Billy asked.

"We really should. Do you know any names right off?"

"Hmm. How about Oliver?"

That Billy just ain't no good at coming up with names.

"Why would we call the world's greatest goat Oliver?"

"Why not?"

"This is a perfect goat, and a perfect goat deserves a perfect name."

We thought about it some more and the perfect name came to me: Courage.

Billy liked the name a whole lot, too.

I got ready to take Courage home when Billy wanted to know if I wanted to take the baseball home with me to sleep with tonight and I said no.

"I'm going to sleep with Courage tonight and I don't care what Mommy says neither."

I got to the house right before supper, and me and Courage went up on the porch and I seen an empty box of candy setting there on the porch rail. I just didn't know which one of my sissies ate it.

I went inside and Courage followed me right on into the house.

"You have to stay outside because we don't want to make Mommy mad. I've got to try and convince her to let me keep you, and you're being inside won't help none," I said.

I went into the kitchen after putting Courage back outside and seen everybody at the table about to eat. Mommy said she was about to come looking for me and wanted to know where I'd been.

"I was over at Billy's playing with Courage."

"Who's Courage?" asked Suzie.

"That's the name of the goat."

Mommy didn't seem to care about the goat any. She seemed like she had other things on her mind, so I didn't push my keeping him as a pet just yet.

Mommy said a prayer over dinner and then we commenced eating.

"Guess what, Price," Mary said.

"What?"

"Mr. Ned asked mommy on a date!"

"Mary," Mommy said like she was embarrassed. "It's not a date."

"It is so," Mary said back.

I was a bit surprised that Mr. Ned would ask Mommy out on a date being he seems almost as afraid of women as me.

"Where are you all going on your date?" I asked.

"It's not a date, it's just two friends getting together. That's all it is. Nothing else. So stop calling it a date."

"Are you all eating here?" asked Mary.

"They're eating in town," Sally said.

"That's a date," Mary said.

"Mommy's got a boyfriend, Mommy's got a boyfriend!" Suzie kept saying, which made Mommy smile.

"You all just eat and hush."

Mary said, "Mr. Ned sure is handsome."

"He is. Do you think we can trust such a handsome man with our mommy?" Sally asked.

"Mr. Ned is a gentleman, so you don't have anything to worry about," Mommy said.

"I ain't worrying about Mr. Ned," Sally said. "I'm worrying about whether we can trust you, Mommy."

Everyone started laughing, and I thought it was the perfect time to bring up Courage.

"Mommy, can I have that goat as a pet?"

Everyone got quiet for a second, then Mommy asked the question I feared she would.

"You mean that mangy beast that tore my kitchen up?"

"Well, yeah."

"No."

"Please, Mommy."

"We can't afford another mouth to feed."

"You don't have to worry about that. He'll eat anything."

"Well, you got me there, but no," Mommy said.

That's when I got on my knees in front of everybody and said, "Please let me keep Courage as a pet. I'm begging you, Mommy."

"Why do you want that goat so bad for?" asked Mary.

"I have my reasons."

"Are you not going to tell me what those reasons are?" asked Mommy.

"I'd rather not."

Mommy began thinking about it, and I couldn't really get a good feel in which way she was leaning.

"Okay," Mommy said.

That's when I jumped up and hugged her and began kissing her cheeks.

"Thank you, Mommy! Thank you, thank you, thank you! And Billy thanks you, too."

Mommy told me, "I'll let you keep him for a little while to see how it works out. But if he gets into the house like he did last night and messes up everything, it's into the pot. Understand?"

"I understand, Mommy. You won't have to worry none about him. I'll watch him for you. Can I go outside and tell him he can stay?"

"That goat doesn't know what you're telling it," Mary said.

"I know it sounds strange, but I really think Courage knows what I'm saying to him."

"What do you mean Courage?" asked Suzie.

"That what me and Billy named the goat. Can I go out with him now?" I asked, and I probably even gave some pouty eyes when I asked.

"Go on," Mommy said.

"Can I eat outside with him?"

"What?"

"Can I eat outside with him?" I asked her again.

"I guess."

"Sound like Price has a date, too," Sally said with a laugh, but I ignored her and took my plate and ran outside onto the porch, and there was Courage waiting for me. I gave him a big hug and told him he could stay.

He gave me a kiss on the face and I gave him some chicken and taters to eat, and afterwards we put the fishing poles back up to their rightful places without anyone knowing they was stolen to begin with.

I now had me a pet goat that thought it was a dog.

As I was out there with Courage, Sally and Suzie came out. Sally started petting Courage, and Suzie sat down beside him and started petting him, too.

Suzie said he was pretty to be a goat and Sally agreed.

I asked them if that candy Billy got 'em was any good and they said they liked it. They told me that Mommy and Mary ate a few pieces and they liked it. Suzie said that Billy was a good hand at picking out candy.

"Which one of you are going to be Billy's girlfriend?" I asked.

They kind of looked at each other, then Sally said, "We decided while eating the candy that we'd wait a while before we get us a boyfriend. We want to mature a little bit before we start dating, and then maybe someone better looking would come along."

Suzie said, "Tell Billy he's free to get him another girl."

Poor ol' Billy. He didn't want to be free. He wanted him a girl right now.

This morning he had two girls, and tonight he has none. Plus, he's out a box of candy.

Mommy and my sissies went to bed and I told them all good night and went into my room and waited. A few minutes passed by before I thought it might be safe. I went over to my window and popped my head out and started calling for Courage, and he came right over to me. It's like he already knows his name. I then pulled him inside my bedroom through the window while trying to be as quiet as I possibly could.

You know, it's a pretty hard thing to do to pull a goat through a window, and I was afraid Mommy was going to hear me and come in my room and catch me pulling him in, and I knew I'd get a whipping for sure.

But it was worth the risk for this here goat who gave something back to me today that them bullies took, and I'm not just talking about fishing poles either.

Once I got him inside, I brought him over to the bed and lifted him up into it. He laid down and I covered him up with the bed covers and then we both went to sleep.

CHAPTER
THIRTY

THE DAY AFTER

Things got ugly in a hurry this morning. I knew I was in trouble when I woke up and Courage was gone.

I got up and began looking all over the place for him, and I was in a state of panic. Finally I found him. He was in the kitchen going through everything in the cabinets again.

This mess wasn't as bad as the other one he made in the kitchen, but it was bad enough. I told him that he had to go on outside because Mommy would be up at any minute and if she caught you in here we both would be dead.

I got behind that goat and started pushing him toward the back door. I got him going straight for it when all of the sudden he made a quick turn to the right and got around behind me, and then before I knew it, he was pushing me in the back with his horns toward the back door.

I then turned around and grabbed him by the horns and tried to pull him out of the house. I was about to open the back door a little, then he would push on me, making me hit the back door, and it would close again and then I had to do it all over again.

I kept telling that goat that he was going to get us in trouble, but he wanted to play, and he must have thought that kitchen was the perfect place for playing.

As I was pulling on that goat's horns and he was shaking his head like a crazy man and pushing me up against the back door while I was pleading with him to stop all of his baaing, I heard the scariest thing I had ever heard in my life.

I heard a voice.

I froze. The goat froze. Time froze. Everything froze just to see what would happen.

That voice came from Mommy.

"Why's that goat in my kitchen again?"

"He snuck out of my bedroom–"

That's as far as I got in my sentence.

"Came out of your bedroom?" Mommy shouted. "What in tarnation is he doing in your bedroom?"

I had forgot that I wasn't supposed to say that part.

Well, it wasn't no time before all of my sissies came running into the kitchen to see who would be killed first, me or Courage.

Mary wanted to know why the goat was in the kitchen, and Mommy said because he was in Price's bedroom all night and I guess he got hungry.

Sally said, "You mean Price slept with a goat?"

"Yes I did, and I ain't ashamed of it, either," I said. "This here is a special goat to me and Billy, and we will defend him against anyone that tries to harm him."

"Even Mommy?" asked Sally.

I didn't say anything. Mommy just came over to me and knelt down.

"I don't know what that goat did for you and Billy to make it so special, but you can't keep it in the house. Do you understand?"

"Yes."

"Get it outside."

"That's what I've been trying to do for the past half an hour," I said to her while trying to keep from crying.

"Then you better try harder or I'll boil both of you up in a stew. And Billy, too. Now get to it!"

So I took to my commands in a hurry for everybody's sake, and Courage seemed to finally understand that two lives were at stake here and let me take him on outside. Mommy apparently forgave us because neither one of us became part of a stew.

CHAPTER
THIRTY-ONE

A LESSON

Me, Sally, Suzie, and Courage went fishing after lunch while Mary was giving her piano lessons. Suzie usually doesn't go with us, but she said she would today even though she doesn't have a fishing pole.

We got to our fishing spot and me and Sally started baiting our hooks when Suzie said she wanted to do it. So I gave her my line and handed her a worm. She sat there looking at that worm like she didn't know if she wanted to touch it or not.

"Go ahead and take it," I said.

"It might bite me."

"Worms don't bite. They don't got nothing to bite with," I told her.

Suzie took the worm into her hand and then took the hook in her other hand and speared that worm but good. She said happily, "I did it, I did it! You know, it's a lot like sewing."

I don't know what the big deal about that was - I done it at least a million times.

I gave my line a toss into the river and we all sat there waiting for the fish to start biting.

Sally wanted to know if Mr. Ned was going to be our new daddy, and I didn't exactly know.

Suzie said, "If he marries Mommy, we would all probably move into Mr. Ned's house."

"We'd live on a farm?" I asked.

"I reckon so," said Suzie.

"That would be great. He has a nice farm and they'd be plenty of room for Courage and all."

Sally said, "Your obsession with that goat is disturbing."

"I thought the same thing about your alls obsession with Billy."

"Well, if we do move, maybe you can get you a real dog instead of that goat."

"I don't need a real dog. I have a real goat, and that's all I need."

"A goat ain't no pet," Sally said.

"Well, this one is," I told her.

They looked at each other like they thought I was crazy and then they looked over at Courage, who was chasing after a butterfly.

Sally said, "That goat ain't better than a dog."

"He is so," I said.

Suzie said, "If he's better than a dog, then make him fetch."

Suzie got a stick and brought it over to me.

I took that stick and looked at Courage. I got to saying to myself that goats don't fetch. I knew that goats don't fetch.

Every boy and girl knows that goats don't fetch, and here I was going to show my two loud-mouth sissies that goats fetch.

Suzie and Sally started laughing. This made me mad, so the showdown had begun.

I shouted at Courage to come over to where I was at, but he didn't pay me no mind.

Suzie said, "A dog would come over to you when you call for it. A goat just runs into the kitchen and makes a mess."

"Well, me and Courage has just become pals, so we're still learning about each other. And that rule applies to dogs, too."

I went over to where Courage was and started petting him and then whispered a description of what I've got myself into.

"Now listen, Courage, we have been challenged. And by two girls, at that. So we have to answer that challenge. What I'm going to do is throw this stick and you have to go and get it and bring it back to me like you was a dog. Now, I don't mean that as an insult to the goat community, but I think you understand what I'm saying."

He just looked at me and then turned away.

"Listen now, you have to do this on behalf of all boys that have sissies all over this world. Will you do this for me?"

He sort of made a noise that I didn't understand. I looked over at my sissies and shouted, "Are you two ready to see some serious grade-A fetching?"

"Yeah," Sally said. "Where do we go to see it?"

They started laughing again and I took that stick and threw it and shouted, "Go fetch!"

Courage jumped upon my chest and knocked me down, and I fell into the river. My sissies started laughing so hard that they could barely breathe.

I sort of gave up on fetch, but not on Courage. I just took my fishing pole and fished me some more, and Courage ate some weeds by the river.

I tell you what, I don't reckon there is nothing more depressing in a boy's life than having his sissies laugh at him. I sure did learn a lesson today. Girls are just plain ol' mean.

CHAPTER
THIRTY-TWO

MOMMY'S DATE

I was outside on the front porch while my sissies were inside helping Mommy get ready for her date with Mr. Ned. Well, Mommy still doesn't call it a date, but we all do.

Courage was running around the front yard playing with some empty boxes he found in the wood house. He kept getting them stuck on his head and I had to keep going out there and chase him around the yard trying to get 'em off. I felt like a dang fool chasing him around like that, but if I didn't get that box off of his head, he'd run smack dab into something or suffocate and die right there in the yard, and I'm pretty sure that nobody wants to die with a box on their head. Goats included.

As I was sitting on the porch, I seen Billy walking up the road. He was carrying another present with him. It dawned on me that he was bringing another box of candy, and he doesn't even have any girlfriends to give it to now.

Billy said, "I brought some more candy, I just don't know who I'm supposed to give it to."

Well, he no sooner said that when Courage came over and knocked him down onto the ground. That crazy goat had done and got another box stuck on his head and he couldn't see where he was going and ran smack dab over poor ol' Billy.

I got down there to where Billy was laying and asked him if he was okay.

Billy said, "Why's Courage running around the yard with a box on his head for?"

"I don't really know. I just guess it's something that goats do."

Billy said, "It looks like he's trying to play hide and go seek with himself."

"Well, I don't know what he's doing, but he seems to be enjoying himself."

"You know that I have an aunt that used to run around the house with a flower pot on her head yelling at the top of her lungs, 'Look everybody, I'm an onion!'"

"Why would she do that for?"

"I don't really know. I reckon every family has a goat in it, and she was ours."

Billy then got up and picked up his present and dusted it off. When he bent over, I could see that he had some comic books in his back pocket all rolled up.

"What do you have there?"

"Present for my girl."

"I mean in your back pocket."

"Oh, I brought some more Batman comic books for you to look at."

We went over and sat on the porch and I got to looking at them comic books while Billy just sat there with the present in his lap. He even had on a bow tie. He kept looking at the front door like he was expecting somebody to come out.

At that point, I knew I was going to have to tell him that no one was going to come out and date him. I put down that comic book and said, "Billy, I've got something I need to tell you."

"Fire away, Price."

"Sally and Suzie decided they wasn't going to get a boyfriend right now. They said they wanted to mature some first. And that might take about three thousand years to happen."

I could see the life just run out of Billy and onto the ground when I told him that.

"Was it because I'm ugly?"

"They just said that they wanted to mature some. That's all. Your ugliness had nothing to do with it."

We didn't say anything after that. We just watched Courage run around the yard with a box on his head.

"Do you want some candy?" Billy asked.

"Yeah," I told him.

So me and him ate that whole box of candy and read comic books all evening, so when it was time for supper I was none too hungry. Billy then headed on home, but he told me that I could keep the comic books for a few more days.

Mommy was running around trying to fix supper for us while she was getting ready for Mr. Ned to come by and pick her up for their date or business meeting or whatever she's calling it.

Mary kept saying that she'd take care of supper and told Mommy to just get ready for Mr. Ned. Mommy said she wasn't going to let her babies starve while she was out on the town eating a good supper.

I tried to tell Mommy that I wasn't very hungry to start with, but I don't think she heard nary a word that I said.

I've never seen Mommy like this before. She seemed pretty nervous. She was knocking things over and dropping things. She sort of reminded me of Courage running around the yard with a box on his head.

We all began eating, except for Mommy, when we heard Mr. Ned's truck pull up in front of the house. We looked at Mommy and she looked at us.

"I can't do it," she told us.

"What do you mean you can't do it?" asked Mary. "All you have to do is eat."

"I'll make a fool of myself."

"Mr. Ned spent all day getting ready for this date, so you have to go through with it or you'll hurt his feelings," said Mary.

I reckon that sort of pulled on Mommy's heart strings, and she nodded. Then Mr. Ned knocked on the door and Mommy turned to Mary and asked, "What do I do?"

"You wait here and I'll get the door," Mary said.

At this point I pushed my plate away because I wasn't about to eat another bite tonight after eating that box of candy. Mommy wanted to know if I was sick and started feeling on my forehead.

"I ain't sick. I'm just full of candy, and it's Sally and Suzie's fault."

"How's it our fault?" asked Sally.

"Because Billy came by to bring his girl some candy, but I had to tell him that he didn't have a girl, so he became depressed and then we ate that whole box of candy."

"Why did you tell him that for?" asked Sally.

"Because you two told me you was going to mature first so you didn't want any boyfriends."

Then Suzie said, "You had no right to tell him that since he brought us some candy."

At that point, Mary walked in and told Mommy Mr. Ned was waiting for her. So everybody ran into the piano room to have a look at Mr. Ned.

He was all dressed up and he said hello to us and we all helloed back. Mary noticed that Mommy was still in the kitchen, so she went to get her and found her washing the dishes.

"What are you doing?" asked Mary.

"I'm washing the dishes."

"Now?"

"They're dirty."

"I'll do the dishes."

"I can't do this."

"Yes, you can. Just let him take the lead."

"I beg your pardon?"

"You know what I mean," said Mary. "Just relax and have fun."

"I beg your pardon."

"Mommy, go."

I heard all of this from the piano room. Our walls ain't too good.

Mommy and Mary came out of the kitchen and we all stood in the piano room not really knowing what to say or do.

"Doesn't Mr. Ned look nice, Mommy?" Mary asked.

"Yes. You look nice."

"You look nice, too," Mr. Ned said to Mommy.

At some point I was assuming that the date would take place away from the piano room, but I was beginning to wonder.

Finally Mary sort of pushed them out of the piano room and toward the front door. Then Mommy stopped and gave us all a big hug like she was going off to war.

"I cherish you all," she said.

We all just sort of looked at each other wondering what in the world she was talking about. Then they left.

Mommy got back to the house around ten o'clock, and we was all waiting in the piano room for her.

"How did it go?" Mary asked.

"Good," she said.

Since I had never been on a date before, I thought I might learn me something that I could use one day, so I listened good.

"Where did you go?" Mary asked.

"The diner near the Movie Palace. Then we went for a walk about the town and sat and talked and then he brought me home."

"That was it?" I asked.

"Yeah."

"Are you going out with him again?" Mary asked.

"Yes."

"When?"

"Next week."

"Did he try to kiss you?" Mary smiled.

"Absolutely not," Mommy said like she would have switched him if he tried.

"Not even a little bit?"

"Mary, what kind of dating have you been doing?" asked Mommy.

"The fun kind," said Mary.

"I think we should have our Bible reading now," Mommy said.

So that's what we did. We had our Bible reading, said our prayers, and headed out to the toilet, and then we went to bed. You know, the Mullins way.

I don't know much about dating, but it seems to me that if a fellow wants to have fun on a date, he needs to take Mary.

CHAPTER THIRTY-THREE

ANGER IN THE OUTHOUSE

I'm mad! I'm madder than I've ever been in my whole stinking life!

I went to the outhouse and was just sitting there when I noticed one of Billy's Batman comic books laying on the floor. I couldn't believe it. It had several pages tore out of it, and that could only mean one thing: One of my sissies has used the world's greatest superhero to wipe their butt!

I was furious! When I got done with my business, I ran into the house holding Batman and said right there to everybody, "Who wiped their butt with Batman?"

Mommy got mad when I said that and told me I shouldn't be using words like that in the house. Then I showed her the comic book and pointed to the pages that had been ripped out.

Suzie said, "I did it."

"Well, what on earth for?" I asked her.

"It was raining and all of the other books would be wet in the outhouse so I just got the nearest thing in the room, which was Batman."

I knew that wasn't the reason she did it. She did it because me and Billy ate all of hers and Sally's candy and she was going to teach us a lesson. Well, that lesson ain't happening!

"You can't take a book that's not even ours and turn it into toilet paper," I told her. "You can only do that with books you own. Right, Mommy?"

"Probably so," said Mommy.

"Billy's going to be mad about this. First you tell him you don't want to date him, then you wipe your tail with his comic book. That just ain't Christian."

Then Suzie said something I couldn't even comprehend.

"I don't see why you're so upset. It's just a funny book."

"Funny book? It's not just a funny book! It's a comic book! A comic book called Batman! In fact, it's more important than just a comic book because Batman is my hero."

"Batman ain't even real," Suzie said.

"He is to me!"

Suzie took off to her room and slammed the door.

Mommy came over to me and put her arm around my shoulder.

"I'm sorry about what happened," Mommy said. "I don't think Suzie knew how important it was to you and Billy."

"Billy is going to kill me when he finds out what happened to pages ten through sixteen."

"We'll try to make it right with Billy somehow."

"Why do girls drive men so crazy?"

"We try to keep men confused so we can have an easier time at taking over the world."

It all came to a head the next day. We was all out on the front porch when we seen Billy coming up the road.

Sally said, "Suzie, you better run and hide because here comes Billy."

So Suzie took off inside and hid in her bedroom.

I got up and met Billy at the end of the yard. I didn't know what he might do, so I made sure to keep him as far away from the house as possible.

Billy held up a nickel and said, "I'm ready for my piano lesson, and when I'm done, me, you, and Courage can go fishing."

"Yeah, we can do that, but I'm afraid I've got some bad news to tell you."

"I can't take piano no more?"

"Worse than that."

"Am I going to get a whipping? What did I do, Price? Tell me! I'll make it right!"

"No, you ain't going to get no whipping."

"What then?"

"It's about your Batman comic book. Specifically pages ten through sixteen."

"What are you talking about?"

"Suzie used those pages to wipe her butt after going to the toilet."

I braced myself because I had no idea what he might do, but all he did was stand there like he was thinking about something.

"Did you just hear what I said?" I asked him.

"Yeah."

He then had a tear form in his eyes.

"That's a rough way to go, ain't it?" Billy said.

"Yeah it is, Billy. I'm sure he put up a good fight though."

"Well, he is Batman," Billy said.

"We'll all try to make it up to you somehow. Suzie just doesn't understand how important Batman is. She thought he was just a funny book is all. She wasn't up on the classics yet, with her being a girl and all."

Billy sat down on the ground and I sat down beside him.

"What are you going to do?" I asked him.

"I don't know."

It was almost like a death in the family. Batman had been wiped out. Literally. Then I got an idea.

"You know, you might be able to use this to your advantage."

"What do you mean?"

"Suzie owes you a date now."

"What?"

"She can't say no to you now after what she did."

Billy thought it over and began to smile. In fact, he smiled so much I thought he was going to break his face.

"That's right, ain't it? She can't say no after that. She just has to go out with me. It's the gentleman thing for her to do, ain't it?"

"It sure is."

"Can you go get her?"

"I sure will. I'll be back in a second."

So I got up and ran into the house and went over to Suzie's bedroom. I tried to get in, but the door was locked. I knocked on the door and told Suzie to come out, and she said no because Billy might try and beat her up.

"Billy ain't going to beat you up. Now unlock the door so I can tell you something."

She unlocked the door and I went in. Suzie, Mary, and Sally were all in there doing whatever it is that girls do when I told Suzie that Billy wanted to talk with her.

"I'm not talking to him. He'll punch me."

"He ain't going to punch you."

"How do you know that?"

"Because you'd kill him for sure, and he knows it."

"Then what's he want?"

"He thinks you owe him a date."

"What?"

"After what you did to his Batman comic book, you have to date him."

"I'd rather he beat me up."

Mary thought the date was a good idea, and Sally thought it was funny and told her that she would have been better off if she just used a wet magazine that day.

"Why does it have to be a date? Can't I just paint his house or something?"

"The girl that betrays the man doesn't get to pick the punishment. All she can do is accept it."

"That's crazy."

But Mary agreed with me, and so did Sally.

"How many dates are we talking about here?" asked Suzie.

Now, I never really thought about that until then, so I just said the first number that came to mind: ten.

"Ten dates?" Suzie screamed. "But I didn't use ten pages. It can't be more dates than pages."

"You don't decide the punishment. The law does."

"Whose crazy law is this?"

"Mine. I'm Billy's council, so I get to set the laws. Also on this date he's not bringing any present either. You've had your last box of free candy. Nor is he going to bring you a ring."

"I'm not marrying the stooge over a Batman comic book!" Suzie shouted.

"As his council, I will not let him marry anyone from this family because all the women in it are nuts, except for Mommy."

"This is insane!"

"Batman drives a hard bargain, woman!"

I could see that she was starting to steam.

"Tell that Billy Foster that he has to be on the front porch at seven o'clock sharp for the date, and he better have a present for me!"

"He doesn't have to bring you a present because you're the one being punished, not him!"

"The woman makes the dating rules, so now get!" said Suzie.

So I getted.

I went out and told Billy to be here at seven o'clock and that he had to bring her a present. I told him that I didn't think he should have to, but he didn't seem to mind any. In fact, he looked pretty happy about the whole thing. Almost as happy as when I took that box off of Courage's head.

Thing is, while I got Courage out of a box, I may have actually put Billy into one.

CHAPTER
THIRTY-FOUR

BILLY'S DATE

I was laying on the floor in the piano room thinking how we were going to make us a comic book if we can't draw the thing. Me and Billy had the perfect hero and the perfect bad guy, but we needed an artist, and I didn't know of any, nor did Billy.

Suddenly I heard a "Psssstttt."

I first thought I had ripped my pants, but when I looked up I saw Billy standing at the window. I walked over to him not believing what I was seeing.

That Billy was dressed up like he was an attraction at the circus. He had on a bow tie that was pink, a checkered shirt and yellow suit jacket with a white feather in the buttonhole, orange pants, and the pointiest shoes that I have ever seen in my life. His hair was all wetted down and parted in the middle, and he had a present in his hands.

"Well looky at Mr. Sunshine!" I said.

"Cut it out, Price," he told me.

"What are you doing here now for? You've got two more hours before your date starts."

"I got to thinking that I don't know how to date, so I was wondering if you would help me. You know, like a practice date."

"You mean you want me to pretend I was Suzie?"

"Yeah. Well, sorta. You know - well, I don't rightly know, but it could help me out of a jam."

It occurred to me at this moment that the two of us have come a long way from Lightning Man.

Since he looked all pathetic standing outside the window, I decided to help the little fellow out. So I made my voice real high like that of a girl's and said, "I got to go to the toilet. Where's them funny books."

I started laughing real hard, but Billy didn't think it was funny.

"You have to be serious now."

"That's an interesting comment from somebody dressed like that."

"Are you going to help me or not?"

"Okay."

"Don't do the voice."

"Okay, I won't do the voice."

"I guess I should start off with something simple."

"I think so."

"Sure is nice weather we're having."

"Yeah."

"That don't sound right."

"Dating folks always talk about the weather."

"No, I mean the voice. I feel like I'm dating you."

"You want me to go back to doing the high voice?"

"You better."

So I did.

"Sure is nice weather we've been having."

"Yes it is, Billy."

"You look nice."

"Thank you. So do you."

"Should I try to hold her hand now?"

"Am I Price or Suzie?"

"You're Suzie, you idiot! I don't want to hold your hand."

"I don't think so. You might pull back a nub."

"Oh."

"Of course, if that's a good present you got her, maybe she'll just give you a big ol' hug. Or maybe even just plop down into your lap."

That got him grinning pretty big.

"What did you get her?"

"A pop bottle opener."

I told him, "That's a good present. It's functional."

"The candy I had been buying was all sold out, so I went with the pop bottle opener."

"Did you bring her any flowers?"

Billy slapped himself right in the forehead with his open hand.

"Dag nab it! I plumb forgot about getting some flowers. I have done and messed up my date before it even got going good."

"Stop worrying. I know where we can get us some flowers."

I climbed out of the window and we took off into the woods and picked some purple flowers, which Billy thought was a good choice because they matched his socks. We headed back to the house but then disaster struck.

Courage had caught sight of them flowers that Billy was holding and he thought that they was meant for him, and he headed straight for Billy.

He jumped on Billy and knocked him down and then began licking Billy in the face. Billy was trying to get up, but Courage kept knocking him back down.

I finally got Courage off of Billy and pushed him away and then helped Billy get up. I have to say that he was a mess. His hair was every which way and he was covered in dirt and grass stains.

"Where's my pop bottle opener?"

He got into a panic. He couldn't have his date without his pop bottle opener and we had to find it but now.

That's when I noticed that Courage had it in his mouth playing with it. We must have chased that goat all over the yard for nearly half an hour. I have to say that there is nothing harder in this world than trying to catch a goat with a pop bottle opener in its mouth.

But we finally got it, though all the wrapping paper was gone. He wanted to know if I had something to wrap it up in and I told him I'd go look.

I started toward the house to look when I saw Suzie on the front porch waiting for Billy. I asked her, "What are you doing out here now? It's not time for your date yet."

"It's seven o'clock now," she said.

I couldn't believe it! We have done and come up on the hour of destiny for Billy without knowing it. So I ran back to get Billy and told him that Suzie was on the front porch right now so you better commence to dating.

Billy got worried and tried to clean himself up. He tried to wrap the present back up as best he could, and I took my shirt tail and tried to clean him up a little more.

"How do I look?" he asked me.

I couldn't tell him the truth. I just told him fine.

"Will you come with me?" Billy asked me.

"No, I ain't coming with you."

He got down on his knees and begged me to come with him. I do tell if someone had happened by and seen us there, people would have thought he was trying to date me.

"You have to do this on your own."

"But I'm scared."

"This is your chance to prove yourself. You are about to face every fear known to man summed up into one event. It's called date night. Now are you going to man up or ain't you?"

Billy got up off his knees and thought about it.

"I'm going to man up."

"That's a boy."

"And what's more, I'm going to go upon that porch and give Suzie Mullins the hardest dating of her life."

"You go do it."

So he headed off with a hand full of flowers that we scrambled up off the ground and a pop bottle opener. I went on back to my bedroom and thought about Lightning Man some more.

Their date ended at eight. Suzie came in the piano room and we all had gathered around to hear how it went.

Suzie didn't want to tell us at first, but she finally gave in to us.

"I don't really know how it went because he didn't say a whole lot. He gave me some flowers and told me that they was a symbol of my sweetness and then he gave me a pop bottle opener and said it was a symbol of the technological advances in the world."

"What does that mean?" Mary asked while laughing.

"I don't know. I guess it's just a man thing to talk about technology on a date."

"What did he do next?" Mommy asked.

"He read a Batman comic book to me. He'd read some and then show me the pictures and then read to me again."

"Did he try and hold your hand?" Sally asked.

"No. He sat too far away for any hand-holding."

"Are you going to date him again?" Mommy asked.

"I don't know. He didn't say anything else about another date."

Mommy then asked, "If he did ask you out on another date what would you have said?"

Suzie began to grin and she humped her shoulders up and down and Sally began laughing and singing, "Suzie likes Billy!"

Suzie turned red and started grinning, and we all thought it was pretty funny. And on top of all that, Billy had conquered his fear of dating Suzie. I think Batman would have been proud of him.

CHAPTER
THIRTY-FIVE

SPIKE

Me and Billy went to our fishing spot today and talked a little about his dating of Suzie, and he had thought it went okay. She didn't hit him or anything, so that has to be a sign that she likes him a bit. I asked him if he was going to date her again, and he said he couldn't until he got his dating clothes all cleaned.

That's when we noticed that an old black man was sitting in our spot doing him some fishing. Billy looked at me and asked, "What do we do now?"

"I don't know."

"I don't want to get thrown into the river again. I sure wish we brought Courage with us. He'd be able to handle him."

I stared at that man and said, "He don't look like he'd throw us in the river none."

"What if he kills us and throws us into the river?"

"I guess we'd just float downstream because if we was dead, we don't have much say in the matter."

"I think we should leave."

That's when I put my foot down. "No, Billy. I felt rotten after I didn't stand up to them boys, so I'm going to do my standing now."

"I prefer feeling rotten to dead," Billy told me.

Then I thought up an idea. "I'll just go down there and ask him if we can fish beside him."

"Okay. But I'm staying here."

So I headed down there to where that man was at. I was a little nervous at first, but when he turned around he seemed right friendly. He told me that he'd be happy for me and Billy to come down and fish with him. So I hollered up at Billy to come on down and he did.

The man shook my hand and then he shook Billy's hand and asked us what our names was.

"I'm Price Mullins and this is Billy Foster."

"What's your name, Mister?" Billy asked.

"Running Goose."

"Running Goose?" I asked him to make sure I heard him right.

"It's Indian for 'I don't know what to call this stupid kid.' "

I think he was just making that up, but he told us we could just call him Spike, so that's what we did.

He said, "I've been here all morning, but all I caught was one trout."

"What have you been using for bait?" I asked.

"Baloney."

"I've never used that as bait before. Me and Billy just use worms."

Spike said, "That's probably best, because my baloney keeps flying away. I try to keep the lid on the bucket, but they keep gettin' out and baloneying over everything."

Me and Billy looked at each other wondering what he was talking about.

Billy asked him, "Do you live around here?"

"I'm from an Indian reservation in South Dakota."

"You don't look like an Indian," Billy said.

"I'm from the dark side of town."

"Did you fight cowboys?" I asked.

"We didn't do a whole lot of fighting. We just mostly roasted watermelons by the fire and sold onions teepee to teepee."

"I didn't know you could roast watermelons." Billy said.

"You can if you have a strong stick."

"What was the name of your Indian tribe?" I asked.

"That Crazy Bunch of Indians That Roasts Watermelons on Sticks."

"Did you all eat anything else besides watermelons?" I asked.

"We tried fish. Two Indians would stand in a river and one would grab the fish with their bare hands, and the other would cut its head off and then the fish would swim away."

"A fish without a head can't swim away," Billy said.

"He didn't cut the fish head off. He cut the other Indian's head off."

"Why did he do that for?"

"Our whole tribe is nearsighted, and we always ended up cutting people's heads off by accident. So we thought it best if we just stuck to roasting watermelons for our eating and leave all the fish alone. Everybody's heads appreciated it, too."

"Why did you come here for?" I asked.

"I'm the only survivor of my tribe. Disease killed everybody else."

"What kind of disease?" I asked.

"Why, indigestion, of course. When a tribe's diet only consists of roasted watermelons, then the end is pretty much written into the story."

"It killed everybody but you?" Billy asked.

"It sure did. The only reason I survived at all is that a herd of ostriches took me in and raised me."

"You were raised up by a herd of ostriches?" I asked.

"Yep," Spike said. "They raised me up until I was nine years old. They taught me love and respect, and I taught them how to fly."

I never heard of an ostrich before, but Billy had, and he said that ostriches couldn't fly none. That's when Spike said that all you needed to fly was a big run ago. He said anything can fly if it had a big enough run ago.

"You're making this up," Billy said, and we both started laughing.

Spike said, "I know it sounds crazy, but it's true. I'll even swear upon the old oak tree beside the moon to prove it's true."

"What did you do after you was nine?" I asked.

"I swam to England to see the Queen."

"From South Dakota?" I asked.

"Yep. I found an underground tunnel and swam through it for forty days and forty nights."

Billy asked, "How did you hold your breath for forty days and forty nights?"

"Mermaids."

"What?" I asked.

"I would swim for a while, and when I needed some air, a mermaid would come over to me and breathe into my mouth and I'd get going again. It was like a kiss of air."

"Mermaids?" screamed Billy. "Are mermaids real? Price, I want a mermaid."

"You can't even handle my sissies, let alone a whole bunch of mermaids," I told him.

"They're topless, ya know?" Spike said.

At that moment Billy's eyes just about exploded. I knew right then and there he was going to go on a mermaid hunt, and God help any mermaid he might find.

That's when I decided to try and change the subject and asked, "What did you say to the Queen when you got over there to her?"

"I introduced myself to her and asked her if there was something she needed me to do. The Queen thought about it for a while and said there was one thing I could do that would please her greatly: She wanted me to make her a cucumber salad."

"That's all she wanted?" I asked.

"Yep. And I even added some ice cream to it to show her how much I respected her, and she ate it right up. All Queens are good eaters."

"Did she like it?" I asked.

"She loved it. In fact, she loved it so much that she made me King for the day."

"What did you do as King?" Billy asked.

"I went fishing."

"What did you catch?" I asked.

"France."

"You caught a country on a fishing line?" Billy asked.

"Yep. Took me two years to reel it in because they eat a lot over there, you know. If they didn't eat so much, I think I could have got it reeled in inside a year, easily."

"What did you do with it after you reeled it in?" I asked.

"I put it back."

"Why?" I asked.

"I didn't really have any need for it. So I put it back and jumped in a barrel and drifted through the Atlantic Ocean to see where I would end up."

"Where did you end up?" Billy asked.

That's when the man pointed at a barrel across the river.

Me and Billy both laughed, and Spike did, too. Now, we didn't believe any of his stories - well, I'm not so sure about Billy - but they sure was fun to listen to.

We didn't catch any fish that day, but we did catch us a friend.

Oh, and Billy did tell me later that when he got growed up that he was going to go looking for some mermaids so they could breathe air into his mouth.

That boy is never going to be the same. And if you ask me, if he ever saw him a topless mermaid, the last thing he'd be thinking about was breathing.

CHAPTER
THIRTY-SIX

THE POSSUM

Excitement! Excitement!

I was in bed sleeping away when somebody woke me up hollering and a-screaming. I wasn't sure at first if I was awake or asleep, but I finally came to the conclusion that I was awake and it turned out I was right.

I got up to try and figure out who was yelling when I noticed it was coming from Mommy's room.

I thought for sure that Courage had done and got into the house and was in Mommy's room trying to get in her bed.

I opened the door and seen Mommy standing up in the middle of the bed screaming.

I asked her what was the matter and she pointed toward the corner of her bedroom. There in that corner was a possum.

I have to say that a possum is just about one of the ugliest creatures that God ever made.

I told Mommy not to worry and walked in and I closed the door so it wouldn't get out, and Mommy started screaming for me to not leave her in there alone, but I knew that if a possum gets scared it plays dead. So I figured I would walk up to it and it would just play dead and then I would pick it up and take it outside and I'd be done with it.

So I went toward it and Mommy told me to be careful, and I told her I would. About the time I got halfway to it, Sally opened the door to see what all the fussing was about, and when she did that the possum ran out the door just as fast as it could.

When it ran out it ran over Sally's feet and scared her to death. She started screaming, which made Mommy start screaming again, and they both started jumping all over me while I tried to get out of the room.

I told them they had to let me go so I could catch that possum, so they finally turned loose of me. I went into the hallway and right quick they slammed the bedroom door closed as hard as they could.

It was obvious that I was on my own in the great possum chase.

I looked for it as best as I could. I turned on some lights hoping that would help me, when suddenly I heard another one of my sissies yelling.

I ran toward their bedroom and seen Suzie in her bed screaming while looking at Mary, who was sound asleep, but that possum was sitting on top of her watching her every move. I told Suzie to stop yelling or she'd wake Mary, but she said she didn't care if she waked the dead.

As the possum sat there, I began to sneak up behind it. But then an unfortunate event took place: Mary woke up.

I tell you what. When Mary seen that possum on her chest looking at her, she let out a louder scream than Mommy, Sally, and Suzie combined.

Mary kicked her covers as fast and as hard as she could, and when she did, that possum went airborne across the bedroom. Now if you think girls are scared of a possum on the ground, you should hear 'em scream when it's in the air.

It so happened that when the possum went flying that it went right out the window. I ran over to the window and looked out and seen it running as fast as it could run to get away from this crazy house full of screaming women.

I told my sissies and Mommy that it was gone and that they could relax. Mommy wanted to know how I got it out of the house, and I told her that Mary kicked it right out of the window.

Sally wanted to know if I thought it would come back, and I said that possum will never come in here again, and I bet he tells all of his possum friends to never come here either because the people that live in this house are a bunch of nuts.

They all laughed and gave me a hug. They said I was their hero.

That's one thing about girls: They can sometimes make a fellow feel pretty big at times. Everybody then went back to bed, and I had a dream about a possum planting corn in a garden.

I don't exactly know why I had a dream about that, but I did. It didn't really make a whole lot of sense to me.

I mean, I understand why I might dream about a possum after trying to get one out of the house, but why in tarnation was he planting corn?

CHAPTER
THIRTY-SEVEN

BRAVE SOLDIER

I was out at the wood house this morning looking around. I wasn't looking for anything in particular, I was just looking around. Mommy calls it boying around.

That's when I seen some old boards and nails piled up, and I got to doing me some serious wondering. Maybe I should build me a treehouse!

I went out and began looking at the surrounding trees for a suitable spot when I seen Billy walking up the road.

He asked me, "What are you doing?"

I told him, "I'm thinking about building a treehouse."

"That sounds great. Do you know how to build one?"

"Nope."

"Well, can I help?"

"Sure. Do you know how to build one?"

"Nope."

We both just stood there thinking we needed smarter friends.

"What do we do first?" Billy asked.

I pondered it and said, "We have to find us a good tree."

So me and Billy headed into the woods looking for a tree. That's when Courage saw us, and he charged toward Billy and knocked him down onto the ground. I don't know what it is about Billy that makes Courage knock him down, but he brings out the craziness in that goat. And it don't take much to do that.

I helped Billy up, and we kept looking for a good treehouse tree. After some serious looking, we settled on a big ol' oak tree. It'd say it stood fifty or sixty feet tall, and we thought this was the perfect spot for the perfect treehouse.

We went back to the wood house and got some boards and nails and a hammer and a saw, and we took it all back to our tree to begin our building.

We both then looked into the top of the oak tree and wondered what we were getting ourselves into.

"It looks a long way up there, don't it?" Billy said.

"It sure does," I told him.

"Are we going to build it in the top?"

"That's where treehouses go."

"Maybe we should build it on the ground."

"It's not a treehouse if it's built upon the ground."

Billy said, "It's not as dangerous either. You know how I'm always falling down. I'd die for sure up there. Besides, we'd never get Courage up in that tree. Courage has to be in our treehouse since he's kind of like our mascot."

"What's a mascot?" I asked.

He told me that it was kind of like a representative of the team. Sort of like a lawyer. Mommy always told me that lawyers belonged in trees so they couldn't harm anybody, so it all seemed to be making sense.

I asked Billy, "So are you saying we should change plans?"

"Yep."

"I guess we'll build us a clubhouse instead of a treehouse."

"I'm all for that."

So we toted all our stuff over to our new spot that was flat and looked like it was a good place for clubhouse building.

I first made me a square out of that lumber that was about ten feet by ten feet. I asked Billy if he thought this would be big enough and he said we should make it bigger. I asked him how much bigger, and he said from here to that big rock over there.

Now, I knew that big rock over there had to be a good one hundred feet from where we was standing, and we didn't have enough lumber to do that unless we tore the wood house completely down and used all of its lumber. There was no way Mommy would allow that, however.

So we decided to just make it about ten feet by ten feet and be done with it. We could add on to it later if we needed.

I guess we worked on that thing all morning, but it wasn't looking like I was thinking it would. We did get the walls up, sort of, anyway. I had the posts up along with some boards nailed to it, but it slanted to the right a pretty good bunch.

I told Billy that it looked like it was going to fall down and he said he thought it looked great. He said when he got home he might build him a little cabin like this.

"But don't you think it's slanted too much?" I asked.

"The reason it's slanted like that is because it doesn't have a roof on it. Once we put a roof on it, it'll be fine."

"I think if we put a roof on it it'll slide right off."

"It'll be fine," Billy said. "You'll see. What are we going to name it?"

I got to be honest, I never really thought about naming it.

"How about The Wonka House?" asked Billy.

"No. That's dumb."

"It's the first thing that come to my mind."

"You got a strange mind," I told him.

"I'd probably think of a better name if I had something to drink."

"I think you might be right. You keep working and I'll go to the house and get us something to drink and eat."

I went to the house and got us each a tomato and a glass of water. I put the tomatoes in my pockets and carried a glass of water in each hand. I was worried the whole time that Courage would come running over to me and knock me down, but he didn't.

I got back up to where Billy was, and he was wanting me to hurry up and get where he was standing because he seen something.

He got to pointing and we seen us a deer up in the woods eating. I don't know what it was eating, it was just sticking its nose into the ground and such. Then I noticed it was on the ground, and that didn't seem right to me.

I asked Billy if deer always eat while lying down and he said he didn't know, but this one was. I said that I thought something was wrong with it.

"Do you think it has gone crazy or something?" asked Billy.

"No, but something's wrong with it."

That's when I noticed it try to move. It would crawl on the ground using its front legs, but it would drag its back legs behind it. It couldn't stand up! It looked like it had broke its back or something.

Billy said he was going up there where that deer was to see if he could help it, and I told him that another deer might be in the area and attack him if he went up there.

He said I could stand there and watch for him and let him know if another deer came charging toward him and I said okay.

Billy went up to the deer talking to it, and that deer was scared to death. It broke my heart to see that deer like that.

Billy got up to it and touched its head and tried to pet it, but that deer didn't want anything to do with Billy. It tried hitting him with its front legs and with its small antlers, and Billy had to back off a few steps. Then I went on up to where he was at.

The deer kept trying to get away, and we kept trying to talk to it to let it know we wasn't going to hurt him. We told it that we just wanted to help it.

I took my glass of water and tried to get the deer to drink it. I took a sip of it myself in front of him to let him know it was something to drink. I placed the glass in front of him and held onto it real tight because I was afraid he might knock it out of my hands. But all he did was turn away from the water and tried to get away again.

Billy said, "He's not going to make it, is he?"

"I don't think so."

"This is sad," Billy said while tears started rolling down his face. "We have to do something."

"We're trying."

The deer stopped moving and was breathing pretty hard. It looked like it was about to just give up on life. So I bent over him and began whispering softly to him that everything was going to be okay in hopes that would try and calm him down and poured some of the water into my hand and offered it to him and this time he began drinking it.

I gave him some more, and before we knew it, that deer had drank all my water and then drank Billy's water, too.

Why, even Courage came up to that deer and licked him in the face like he knew it was in some serious trouble and needed some encouragement.

I decided to go back to the house and tell Mommy what we found, and maybe she would know what to do. She came back with me up into the woods to have a look. Then Sally and Suzie came, and then Mary and her piano class came up into the woods, too, to see the deer.

Suzie said it was sure sad to see that deer like that. I asked Mommy if they was something we could do, and she said she was afraid not.

She said it had broken its back or something and that it was probably going to die. But I couldn't just leave it like this and asked Mommy ain't there's something we could do? Anything at all?

She just said all she knew to do is try to feed it, but she didn't know if that would help or not.

Me and Billy tended to the deer while everybody else went back to the house. We sat there beside the deer and talked to it and petted it. We just felt so helpless sitting there.

I told Billy I was going to go back to the house and get some more water for it, and Billy told me to hurry because he was afraid it might die while I was gone and he'd be here by himself and he wouldn't know what to do.

So I told him I'd hurry, and he said he'd pray for the deer. So he started praying and I started running back to the house to get some more water.

This time I brought a pitcher of water, and when I got there it was still alive. I sat the pitcher down and poured some water into my hands for it to drink. It took a little but then turned away. Billy took out his handkerchief and dipped it into the water and began wiping the deer off with it.

Then the deer laid its head down on the ground and we knew this wasn't a good sign, but we stayed with it. About two o'clock, the deer died.

He was breathing real loud one second and he wasn't breathing at all the next. You could tell he was dead by just looking at him. No movement, no nothing.

I seen Billy trying to hold back tears, and to tell you the truth, I was struggling to do the same.

I told Billy I'd go down to the wood house and get a shovel and we'll bury him. Billy didn't say anything, he just nodded.

I asked him if he was going to be okay and he nodded again. Then I took off, and when I was out of sight I could hear Billy break down crying.

Me and Billy buried him not too far from where we was building our cabin. We was going to bury him right where he died, but the ground was too rocky, so we had to move him to another spot.

Billy said he wanted to call the deer Brave Soldier, and I thought that was a good name.

I took a flat rock and scratched the name on it with a small rock and used it as a headstone. We placed some flowers on the grave and then sung *Amazing Grace*.

Neither of us felt like doing anything else for the rest of the day, so we just headed on back home.

I've been wondering what it was like to die. What does it feel like? Will I be scared or will I be brave like that deer? I don't know.

But one day Mommy is going to die, and I don't want that to happen. I don't want to face that day, but I know I'll have to; there is no way of getting around it. I'm going to have to bury people that I love, and I just don't want to do that.

It almost makes a person want to spend their entire life alone.

CHAPTER
THIRTY-EIGHT

A NEW DAY

I was out feeding Courage this morning when I saw six rabbits sitting in the yard eating grass. I sat and watched 'em for a while, and they didn't seem to pay any attention to me whatsoever. I guess that's a pretty good indication that they were girl rabbits.

I was afraid that Courage would run over there where they was at, but when you put food in front of Courage, his tail could be on fire and he wouldn't notice.

Them rabbits sure was cute. Of course, when Courage got done eating, he seen them sitting out there in the grass and he was off like wet on rain to catch 'em.

All he wanted to do was play, but them rabbits took off just as fast they could, and Courage had no chance of catching 'em either. So Courage stopped in the yard and watched 'em all bolt off into the woods. Then Courage turned and ran toward me and knocked me onto the ground and began licking me in the face like I was a cherry sucker.

I tell you one thing, being licked in the face by a goat that has just ate leftover mashed potatoes for breakfast is something you will never forget.

I then headed back into the house and seen Mary washing dishes and asked her where Mommy was.

"She's got a job at the hospital for the next week or so."

I was stunned. I didn't even know she wasn't in the house.

"Why didn't anyone tell me?" I asked.

"Because no one had to," said Mary.

That comment sort of defined my life pretty good, I thought.

Mary said that Mommy was in town yesterday delivering some of her sewing to the store to sell when she heard that they needed some help at the hospital, so she walked over there and checked in on it and they said she could start tomorrow.

"But she ain't a nurse," I said.

"She's not trying to be a nurse, you nut," Mary told me. "She's just cleaning up the place, is all. She said it might be hard work, but she's cleaned up after us our whole lives, so she might as well clean up for other people and get paid for it."

"How much do they pay?" I asked.

"Doesn't matter," she said. Just as long as they pay, and the Lord knows we need money."

I have to admit that I felt pretty bad about this. I think I should be doing all the hard work around here and Mommy should be taking it easy. It seems like mommies always have to do more than they should.

So everybody pretty much went about our day even though it felt odd not to have Mommy in the house.

Mary had piano practice set up, and her jar that she keeps all of her nickels in is just about full. We asked her what she was going to do with all that money, and she didn't rightly know yet, but she'd get something for herself and then help pay some bills and such.

I think Mary is getting to be a better piano player every day. All that practicing, I reckon. Of course, I think Billy gave her a run for her money, so she thought she should try and be a better player. It ain't good when the student is better than the teacher, yet he pays the teacher a nickel to make him better.

As I got my hammer and some nails that I kept in the wood house, I started heading up to the building that me and Billy started, and then here came Sally and Suzie.

"What are you going to do with that hammer?" asked Suzie.

"I'm going to work on my building," I told 'em.

"Can we help?" asked Sally.

"They ain't no girls allowed in mine and Billy's clubhouse."

"I bet Billy would allow us to help," said Sally.

"No, he won't. We're buddies, best buddies, I'd say, and he knows that girls aren't allowed in the clubhouse."

"Here he comes now," said Suzie. "So we can up and ask him."

They both ran toward Billy as fast as they could, and I knew right then and there that I needed to try to head 'em off at the pass.

Billy seen my sissies running toward him and he sort of just stopped where he was and didn't know rather to head off into the other direction or open his arms up just as wide as he possibly could to give 'em a big hug.

He sort of did neither as I tried to catch up to him as fast as I could. When I got to where he was standing, my sissies were already asking him about helping with the clubhouse.

"Can we help you and Price work on your dollhouse?" asked Suzie.

"It ain't a dollhouse!" I shouted. "It's a clubhouse! For men! A lodge even."

"A lodge?" asked Billy. "I like the sound of that. Makes me feel very regal."

"What's regal?" asked Sally.

"Fancy," said Billy.

"Can we help you be fancy?" asked Suzie.

"Well, I don't–" Billy couldn't even get his words out as my sissies kept blabbing.

"We like watching you work," said Sally. "It's very manly."

"And look at Billy's muscles," said Suzie as she grabbed him by the arm and started squeezing it. "They're big, aren't they Sally?"

Sally squeezed Billy's other arm and said, "They are big. Not as big as Mary's, but they are big."

The look on Billy's face when my sissies was squeezing his arms made me know that I was going to have girls working on my lodge today.

"I don't see why you all can't help us," said Billy. Then he added, "The more the better, right Price?"

I stayed cold to his question.

My sissies stuck their tongues out at me then headed up to the clubhouse. Billy watched 'em head up with a big grin on his face, then he looked over at me.

"They think I'm manly."

"That's because they don't know you like I do."

Then I punched him in the arm.

"Come on, lover boy."

"What's wrong, Price?"

"I didn't want them girls up there. They'll ruin everything."

"But the more people that help us, the quicker it'll get done."

"They ain't coming to help, they're coming to spy."

"Spy?" Billy asked. "Spy for what?"

"They's my sissies and they want to make my life miserable."

"Having your sissies around don't make me feel miserable. Makes me feel all - you know - tingly."

"Tingly?!"

"Yeah, tingly," Billy said.

"I'll tingly you!"

"Don't hit me!" he shouted as he turned around real quick like with his hands up over his face.

"I'm not going to hit you."

"I didn't know you didn't want them up there with us."

"Would it have mattered?"

"Not really."

I have to say that I almost smiled when he said that, but I held it back the best I could.

So the two of us headed up to the clubhouse, which has become polluted with girl smell, and began working on it with our hammering and laying everything out.

I had three hammers up there because I kept forgetting to take one back, and when I went to looking for it, I couldn't remember where it was and thought I lost it so I'd scrounge up another one and then find the stupid thing up at the clubhouse where I had left it. It's like I can't remember anything anymore, so I have to write everything down and then I can't read the crazy thing. Makes a boy want to bust, although my forgetting did give us an ample supply of hammers for everyone.

Well, we went about our hammering, and that's when I learned something big time. That thing being that girls can't hammer worth a lick.

They bent more nails than anybody I had ever heard tell of. That's when they weren't missing it completely. Why, Suzie took one big swing with her hammer and it swung out of her hand and hit poor ole Billy right in the shin. He started rolling around on the ground holding his shin. Serves him right, I'd say. Of course he was okay after a minute or so and Suzie said she was sorry and Billy told her not to worry about it and that if he had ever had to get hit in the shin with a hammer he was glad it was from her.

That boy is nuts when it comes to my sissies.

We did get a pretty good chunk of clubhouse building done today, and though my sissies took forever in their hammering, they was still good helpers. Not many sissies in this world would help their brother out like that, though I don't think their actions was pure.

As the day was coming to the end, Billy called me over to the other side of the clubhouse and began whispering to me.

"Will you ask Suzie if I can date her on the front porch again?"

"Why don't you ask her?"

"I can't ask her."

"Why not? She's standing right over there."

"She might say no and then I'd feel all depressed and everything."

I told him, "She almost killed you with a hammer, Billy. The least she can do is date you on the front porch."

"I don't want her to date me simply because she feels guilty about almost killing me. I want her to date me because she wants to date me. Otherwise I'm wasting my time."

I shook my head. "Okay, I'll ask her for you."

"Thanks, Price. I'll stay over here in case she reaches for another hammer."

I can't believe the things I do for that boy.

So I headed over to Sally and Suzie, and they were whispering something, but once I got over there they stopped.

"What are you two whispering about?" I asked.

"Stuff," said Sally.

"What stuff?"

"Girl stuff," Sally replied with a giggle.

"Well, I'm here to talk about Billy stuff."

"Talk on," said Suzie.

"He wants to know if he can date you on the front porch again."

"If Billy wants to date me on the front porch, then he's going to have to walk all the way over here and ask me to date him on the front porch like a proper gentleman."

She said it loud enough to where Billy could have heard her. Shoot fire, they could have probably heard her in China.

Then Sally said, "I might let him date me on the front porch, but he'll have to bring me a present. A big one."

That's when Suzie picked up the hammer and began driving a nail, and Sally went and got another board, and I looked at Billy and he looked at me and we both humped our shoulders not knowing what to do.

Now, to be honest, I don't think either one of 'em thought Billy was that great. They just wanted to get some presents on the front porch was all.

So I decided that the best thing to do was to get them both a boyfriend or at least access to another fella so Billy doesn't get plumb worn out from the dating chaos my sissies are causing.

"I got a proposal for the two of you," I said. "How 'bout I get another fella for you two to consider?"

"What fella are you proposing?" asked Sally.

"Bobby Sweetwater."

"Who?" they both asked with their noses turned up so high that if it had rained they'd both drowned right there in front of me.

"Bobby Sweetwater," I said again.

They still had no idea who I was talking about.

"He was in my class. You've both seen him before. The teacher had to help him get that rock out of nose after he put it up in there."

"Why did he do that for?" asked Suzie.

"I reckon cause it was a Tuesday. I don't know. But that's not the point."

"I'm not dating any fella on our front porch that put a rock up his nose on purpose, then had to get the teacher to get it out for him," said Sally. Suzie nodded in agreement.

"He was just having an off day, is all. We all do something crazy in our life which ends up with us laying down on our back and having someone using a bobby pin to try and get something out of us. It's the way of the world," I said, not half believing what I was saying.

"You're asking way too much from us," said Sally. "We ain't that desperate for a man. We got our standards."

"Standards? You're dating Billy, for crying out loud," I told 'em.

"I can hear you, Price," said Billy.

"Sorry, Billy. I didn't mean you any harm there," I told him.

That's when Billy walked over to where we was having our discussion.

"I'd like to say something," said Billy. "I know Bobby Sweetwater and he's a good guy. I don't want you all to define him by that nose incident."

"So you're saying we should dump you and start dating him?" asked Sally.

"Well, I thought maybe just one of you would dump me and the other one would keep me," said Billy.

My sissies looked at each other and then walked away from us and started whispering. I looked at Billy and he looked at me, then we looked at them and they came back to where we were doing our looking.

"We don't like your idea," said Sally.

"What do you mean you don't like the idea?" I shouted. "It's the only idea that makes any sense. One of you gets Billy and one of you gets Bobby. That's the way the world is supposed to work."

"No. We like watching the boys fight over us."

"I don't want to fight anyone," said Billy. "Me and Bobby are friends."

That's when trouble came running into Billy shaped like two crazy girls.

Sally got up in front of Billy and kissed him right on the jaw, and then Suzie did the same thing, and then they both just up and left.

Billy stood there a bit dazed and then he looked over at me and said, "I've got to kill Bobby Sweetwater."

My sissies have created a monster, and I'm going to have to start toting around a bunch of rags to clean up the blood, and I just might have to keep a bobby pin on hand just in case.

I tell you the truth, having to live in a house full of girls will curl your toenails black.

CHAPTER THIRTY-NINE

THINKING ON STUFF

Me and Courage headed down toward the river looking for junk. I thought maybe I could find something that had been washed up on the riverbank that I could use to put on or in our clubhouse.

I've been thinking a lot about my clubhouse today, and I don't like the name of it. I think it should have another name. Something with dignity. So I began thinking me over some ideas to name it and came up with "The Lodge."

I kind of liked the name because it sounded important, and like Billy said the other day, it sounded fancy.

I could say something like, "Well, I guess I'll head on up to The Lodge and do my writing. Maybe read me some comic books."

Then it hit me that I could make it my writing cabin. Maybe I can put me a woodstove in it for the winter so I wouldn't freeze to death. I don't think Billy would mind any if I used it for writing.

Yeah, I like how that sounds, you know, important like. It also sounded like something a man would say, you know, "I'm going to The Lodge tonight, so don't wait up for me." In fact, the more I thought about it the more I liked it.

I told Courage that I was going to call my writer's cabin The Lodge, but he didn't seem too impressed by it. I think it's because he's been hanging around my sissies too much.

Some good news about Billy and Bobby Sweetwater. They won't be fighting for the hearts of my sissies. Bobby and his family moved a few weeks ago so that his daddy could find work. Billy said he found it out when his mom was helping him get his foot out of a coffee can that he had got it stuck into. I don't know how Billy did that, but I think that was pretty good proof that he had lucked up on not getting killed by trying to fight someone.

As me and Courage was walking down the road, I would look down at the river to see if I could find something down there that I could use for The Lodge - or for anything, for that matter. I always like looking for stuff and see if I can use it somehow to make my life more tolerable. A tolerable life is essential with three sissies.

That's when I seen something sticking out of the river, so I went down there where it was to look it over. I come to find out it was a bread box made of tin. So I got a stick and was able to pull it over to where I was standing, and I gave it a good look over and wondered if I should keep it or not. I could probably clean it up and store my journal in it or something like that. So I decided to keep it and if I found something better I could put down the bread box and take the other thing, so I began looking some more.

I seen an old board in the river stuck between two rocks. It was damming up the water, so I thought I would go and un-dam it. After all, that's what boys do.

I walked on some rocks that were sticking out of the water and grabbed the board and lifted it up and then fell right into that water. Fell right on my back and on them hard rocks, too. It was a good thing they weren't sharp or they would have went clear through me. Of course, even though they didn't spear me, their solidness still hurt. And if you ever fall into the river, your first reaction is to get up out of it.

And that's what I did. I stood up as fast as I could and looked over the situation. If I had just ignored the dam, none of this would have happened. But that's when I saw something interesting.

I first thought it was a board, but it was a piece of metal. A big piece at that, and I pulled it up and got to looking at it real good and saw it was a Coca Cola sign. The biggest one I had ever seen. I thought I could use that on my lodge roof to keep the rain out. I think Mr. Coca Cola would approve.

This was turning out to be a pretty good day for junk hunting. How many people can find their roof in the river? Not many, I'd say.

So I put that tin sign on the bank to dry some, and I was able to get it right in the sun so it would dry pretty quick. As I was waiting for it to get good and dry, I laid down beside it and looked up into the sky and seen some big fluffy clouds cross overhead and I got to thinking about Lightning Man.

Now, I haven't been working much on my comic recently, but I got to thinking about him pretty big-time now. Maybe the clouds gave me some sort of inspiration. Mrs. Collins told me that writers sometimes get their inspiration to write from things around them, and apparently fluffy clouds do it for me. I don't know if that makes me a real writer or just strange.

As I thought about Lightning Man a little more, I thought he could help sell Coca Cola. I mean, it happens all the time with cartoon characters selling stuff to people, you know, like that Mickey Mouse feller. So why couldn't Lightning Man do the same thing? He might make me and Billy a pretty big pile of money. Who wouldn't want to get in on the ground floor of the greatest comic book hero that had ever lived? They'd be crazy not to.

I'm going to have to tell Billy about my plan, but first I'm going to have to write me a Lightning Man story. Something that will even be better than Batman, and that's going to take a lot of work on my part because I don't know if anything is better than Batman.

Maybe Lightning Man could even have his own radio show. Coca Cola could be the sponsor of the show, and maybe I could be the voice of Lightning Man. Hey, that sounds perfect. Lightning Man's secret identity could be Price Mullins. Hey, yeah! Price Mullins, by day just an ordinary zillionaire, but by night he turns into Lightning Man, protector of all the people in the big city of Coca Cola Land.

Of course, if Coca Cola won't sponsor the show, we'll have to call the city something else.

I have to say, I think these are pretty good thoughts.

CHAPTER
FORTY

AN EXCERPT FROM LIGHTNING MAN

Price Mullins was no ordinary zillionaire. Though extremely handsome and successful, with at least one hundred women every day proposing marriage to him, he had a higher calling. That calling was his city, Gorilla Lake.

Price Mullins had seen his beloved city taken over by the mob, which destroyed the will of every person in the city to live.

He wanted to do something about it, but what could one man do?

His life changed on September first 1941. He was out doing his zillionaire things when he was suddenly struck by lightning. He was knocked out for what may have been days, but no one came to his aid because he was in the woods when it all happened.

When he woke up, he noticed something was very different about himself - he was glowing from head to toe.

He got up and he was scared. Then he looked at his glowing hands, and when he clinched them into a fist, he felt something pulsing inside them. He took his fists and pointed them outward like Superman does when he flies, and lightning shot out of them.

He didn't understand what was happening, but instead of being afraid of what he had become, he decided to embrace it.

He got to thinking about his beloved city, Gorilla Lake, which he thought was a pretty good name for a city, and he decided right then and there that he was going to take on crime himself.

He then began to practice with his new powers to learn how to control them. He could shoot flames out of his fists and burn down a tree, and he learned that if he concentrated real hard he could actually hurl fireballs from his hands into the sky that exploded like fireworks. It made for interesting times.

He did burn down his bed by sneezing, which he didn't mean to do, but he also learned that he could touch a red hot stove and it wouldn't burn him. He could actually cuddle it. Though he made sure no one was watching when he did that.

After weeks of practicing all of his powers and learning their good sides and bad sides, one night he was going for a walk to think over what had happened to him when he seen a beautiful white horse in a field. The horse walked over to him and he instantly knew that the horse was going to help him fight crime. He decided to call it Weiner.

He also decided to be a superhero and made his red, white, and blue costume from scratch. Actually he had his mommy do it because she was a good sewer. He didn't tell her what it was for. He didn't have any sissies, so he was pretty pleased.

One day the bank was robbed and he knew as well as everyone else in the city that the gangster everyone calls Stomachs (he was called that because he ate a lot) did it. So he rode Weiner up to Stomachs' large mansion and charged inside shooting lightning bolts from his fists in every direction to kill all the bad guys.

Then he rode up to where Stomachs was lying on the floor, and his horse stood over him with his front legs up and Lightning Man said, "Don't move or my Weiner will kill you."

Then the police was called and Stomachs was arrested, and people began to learn of this new hero that was protecting their city and everyone was proud, and for the first time in a long time that actually felt safe.

The End.

I've got to come up with another name for the horse.

CHAPTER
FORTY-ONE

SHOWING BILLY MY STORY

Well, today I thought I'd show Billy my story. I had spent a good few hours on it last night and thought he might like it, but it turned out to be a big waste of time because all he would say was, "Weiner? Why are you calling the stupid horse Weiner for?"

"It's just the first draft, Billy. I didn't want to stop my flow until I got done. I'm going to go back over it again," I told him.

"You're messing this all up," he said. "All you had to put in it was 'X.' You didn't have to name him now."

"What's the big deal?" I asked him.

"Because every time I look at this horse I'll know he was originally called Weiner and that just makes it all seem silly."

"It's not silly. Writing is hard work, and I'm doing the best I can."

"Why's he on a horse for anyway? He should be flying. If a man can shoot fire out of his fists, then he should be able to fly."

"Batman doesn't fly," I said.

"You're not writing Batman. You're writing Lightning Man."

At that point I knew he was right. I was trying to put too much of Batman into my comic book, and if I do that he can't stand out from all the other comic books. I was going to have to make me some changes.

"Besides," Billy said, "I can't draw a horse."

"You're going to be tracing the drawings, so what does that matter?" I asked.

"I don't have any comic books with a horse or spaceships, for that matter."

"Well, how in tarnation are we going to have a good comic book without horses and spaceships?" I asked him in a rather loud voice.

"Maybe we just ain't going to have us a comic book!" he replied in an equally loud voice.

"They'll be a comic book if I have to trace the drawings myself!" I yelled back.

"Well, you can't do that because you don't have any comic books to trace over."

"What do you mean?"

"I'm taking 'em all home with me and you can't stop me none neither."

"Take 'em all then! I don't care!"

"I will, thank you very much!"

And he up and did it right there in front of me. Took 'em every one home with him. I was as mad as I could get. Then

I watched him walk on out of the house carrying all of them comic books and I just watched him go farther and farther away down the road.

That's when all of my anger turned into sadness. They were gone. All the comic books that he had was gone, and I was left with nothing.

What was I going to do without any more Batman?

I went back into the house and into my bedroom and sat down on the bed and a feeling of depression just washed over me like I had never felt before.

It was a strange feeling. I didn't realize just how important them comic books were to me, and now they was gone and so was my best friend.

Then I started to cry.

CHAPTER
FORTY-TWO

FOOD FIGHT

Mary fixed supper this evening because Mommy was late getting back from the hospital.

"How long is Mommy going to have to work there at the hospital?" I asked.

Mary said, "Hopefully for a while. She's been looking for work and now she's got it. She just can't quit."

"But she's working too late," said Suzie.

"That's her job," said Mary. "If she didn't do it then no one would. Some people have jobs in which they have to work late. We all have to do what we can to make ends meet."

"I wish she didn't have to work so late," I said.

"Well, ain't nothing we can do about it right now. It's the best job she can find so she can't complain about it, and it's not helping to have you all complaining about it either because you'll make her feel bad."

"We don't want her to feel bad," said Sally. "We just want her home."

"If she's home she can't make no money," said Mary.

"Yeah she can. You're home and you make money," said Suzie.

"Not as much as Mommy will. Now you three stop your fussing and get to eating."

Well, about the eating part. Mary was a great sister and all, but she couldn't cook worth a lick. She had fixed us some burnt chicken and something else of which I had no idea what it was. It was burnt something, but that was as far as I could get into trying to figure out what it was.

That's when Sally asked, "What's that thing there?"

Mary said, "You fool, that's cornbread. It's good, too. Best I ever made."

"Then why ain't you eating any of it?" asked Suzie.

"Because I'm trying to watch my figure."

"Maybe you should have watched the stove so it wouldn't have burnt instead," said Sally, which made everybody laugh. Well, except for Mary.

"I've worked on this supper a good long time, and I'm not going to put up with you wise-crackers bad-mouthing my cooking."

"Have you got something in the house we could eat that you didn't have to cook?" I asked.

"I got a balled up fist that you can chew on," Mary said while shaking her fist at me. "Now you all hush up and get to eating or I'll force feed you all some castor oil. Do you all want some of that?"

"What's castor oil?" asked Suzie.

"It's something you get for being mean," said Mary.

"Then you should be taking it then," I said. "Because it's pretty mean of you to try and make us eat your cooking."

"Don't you start on me, Price Wayne Mullins!"

Any time someone calls me by my full name I know I'm fixing to die pretty quick.

"Has Junior ate any of your cooking?" asked Suzie.

"No."

"Don't you think he should?" asked Sally.

"No."

"Why not?" I asked.

"If you all don't hush I'll cook you."

"Well, if you do I hope you don't forget to turn me over so I don't burn like you did to that poor ol' chicken," I said, which was probably going too far, but when someone balls their fist up atcha and threatens to cook ya, then all bets are off, I say.

Suzie and Sally laughed at what I told Mary, which unfortunately for all involved encouraged me to continue on with my fat mouth.

"She's afraid that if Junior ate her cooking then he'd stop dating her," I said.

"You three need to hush about my cooking. I don't need to be made fun of after all the work I did in preparing this for you. I did it because I care for you three. You know that, don't you? And this is the appreciation I get. Well, take this then."

Mary then took a scoop of what I think was mashed potatoes out into each of her hands and threw them at Sally and Suzie, which made me laugh pretty good. I mean she caught 'em right in the face with both throws, and they just sat there with their mouths open in complete shock.

Mary then looked right hard at me and said, "Oh, do you think that's funny?"

I was laughing so hard at this point that I couldn't answer. That's when she picked up the bowl of mashed potatoes and set it down on my head. But I was in such a giggling mood that I just kept on. I mean, I was laughing so hard that I was having a little trouble breathing.

That's when Sally took the mashed potatoes off of her face with her hand and threw it at Mary, and it hit her right in the head. By this time I had done and fell to the floor laughing, which I think got them to laughing, and before I knew it, we had us a full-scale food fight on our hands. And we was having a pretty good time doing it. We was screaming and laughing and just having fun. It must have went on for a good ten minutes or so, and it's a time that I'll never forget.

We did finally stop, though, and the four of us all pitched in and cleaned everything up and then went into the kitchen and cleaned ourselves up before Mommy got home. If she had found out what we did, she would have hung us by a nail for sure. And frontwards at that.

Mary's food ain't much for eating, but it sure throws good.

Mommy got home a little after ten o'clock. Mr. Ned brought her home in his truck. I have to say that before she came we were getting pretty worried about her. She never stayed out this late for work.

When she came in you could tell that she was dead tired. Mary told her to sit down and rest and then gave her some chicken and mashed potatoes, the ones we didn't throw, and do you know that she ate 'em straight down without thinking twice.

I have to say that anybody that can eat Mary's cooking without it bothering them must have been about to starve to death.

I'm writing this down in bed with my lamp on, and I just noticed a lightning bug flying around the room, shining his little tail all about. Wonder why he came in my bedroom. That little fellow could have went anywhere on this mountain, and he chose my bedroom.

I wonder if he had him a good talking to with that possum. That possum probably told him that he could go into my bedroom but don't go into any of those girls' bedrooms because they is crazy.

Yeah, I bet that's what he said. I really do.

CHAPTER FORTY-THREE

ME AND BILLY

After eating breakfast this morning, me and my sissies said goodbye to Mommy as Mr. Ned took her on back to the hospital to work. She had to work late last night and then got up at a little past four this morning and headed back in. I don't understand what she's doing this for. Seems like there's other ways to make some money for the family, and it's starting to bother me that she's doing this and not me.

Suzie and Sally are doing some sewing today of blankets which they were going to try and sell at Junior's daddy's store. Mary has her piano lessons, so she can get some money to come in for the family, and here I am doing nothing.

That's when I noticed a magazine in the living room.

"Where did this come from?" I asked.

Mary came over and looked at it and said, "That's one that Mommy brought from the hospital. She wanted you to look at it and see if you could get some ideas for your writing."

"What kind of ideas?" I asked.

"Story ideas, you nut. They buy stories, you know. So maybe you could sell some to them."

"What kind of stories?" I asked her.

"Anything you can make up, I guess. Just get to work on one and send it in. Maybe you can make you some money."

Mary then headed to the front door because one of her players had come for their lesson, so I took the magazine and rolled it up and slid it into my back pocket and thought I'd go up to my lodge and have me a good look at it.

I grabbed my Coca Cola sign and bread box and started on up when I seen in the distance Billy coming toward me.

I didn't really know what to expect at this point. He was pretty mad when he left the other day, so I was braced for anything.

"Hey, Price."

"Hey, Billy."

"Whatcha doing?"

"I was going to head up to The Lodge," I told him.

"Lodge?"

"That's what I'm calling the clubhouse now. Do you like it?"

"It's got a nice ring to it. What's that you've got there?"

"That's a Coca Cola sign and bread box that I found in the river."

"What are you going to do with it?"

"I'm going to put the sign on the roof of The Lodge, but I don't know what to really do with the bread box."

“You might want to put this in it.”

Billy pulled a comic book out of his back pocket. It was issue one of *The Arrow*.

“What’s this?” I asked in an excited voice.

“My dad got it for me and I wanted to show it to you.”

“Well, I’m sure glad that you did. Where did he get it?”

“He said he found it on the side of the road.”

“You mean someone threw it away?”

“Either that or they just lost it.”

“And they left it there? Man, if I lost this book I’d be searching for it the rest of my life.”

“Me, too.”

“Do you want to head up to The Lodge with me and read these books?”

“What book do you have?”

I pulled out that magazine and showed it to him.

“Scribner’s Magazine? What’s that?” Billy asked.

“They buy stories. I’m going to write me one and send it to ‘em and they’ll pay me.”

“Pay you? Are you sure?”

“I’m as sure as rain.”

Billy’s eyes got big and I knew what he was thinking.

“Can I write one, too?”

That’s what I thought he was thinking.

“I don’t see why not. Ain’t nothing to it.”

“I’ve never really wrote a story before. I’ve made up a few, but only to stay out of trouble.”

“Well, we have to write it down, but we can’t use the paper I’ve been using.”

“What do you mean?”

"I've been using anything I could get my hands on for my journal and for Lightning Man, but to send something to them we'll need paper that's clean on both sides."

"Where are we going to get that?"

"I don't know. But what's more is that we're going to have to type our stories, too. We can't handwrite 'em any."

"I don't have a typewriter or even know where to find one."

"Well, we can write our stories out on any paper first, you know until we get it right, like I did with Lightning Man, but we'll have to type it before we send it."

"Speaking of Lightning Man … " Billy said as he reached into his back pocket and pulled out a folded-up piece of paper and showed it to me.

"I've been practicing drawing horses. You know, for Weiner."

I have to admit that it wasn't a bad-looking horse - once he showed me which way it was facing - but I had to tell him my thoughts on the matter.

"I know you worked hard on it, Billy, but you was right to begin with. They'll be no horse in Lightning Man."

"Are you sure?"

"I'm sure. He's going to fly. No horse needed."

"Okay. That's what we'll do then. Of course, we better not tell my mom what we're up to," said Billy.

"Why not?" I asked him.

"She said that I was getting close to being a man and that men don't waste their time reading comic books."

"Well, if the only way I can be a man is to stop reading comic books then a boy I'll always be."

"Amen, Price. Let's go to The Lodge and get to boying around. Moms don't know everything especially when it comes to men."

"Amen back at you."

We turned and headed up to The Lodge and had our day planned out for the next several hours.

"But I still don't want you to tell my mom what we're doing."

"I won't, Billy."

It don't really matter if you're a little boy or a grown man, you don't always want your mommy finding out what you're doing, and it really don't matter what the finding out is.

CHAPTER
FORTY–FOUR

THE CHAIR

Me and Billy worked on some stories yesterday. I wrote out four of them, but I just didn't like any of them. Billy wrote about a dog that could fly. I don't think Scribner's magazine is going to buy a story like that, but if that's what he wants to write, I guess I can't stop him. But I need to try some more times before I get one strong enough to send.

I got up this morning and went and fed Courage and went on over to The Lodge and began working on that. I still needed some more stuff for the roof and such, though Billy and I have done a pretty good bunch of work on it here lately.

I went on back down to the wood house to find some more tin or something I could use to put on the roof to keep it from leaking in case it rained. I didn't find anything though, so I thought I could walk along the railroad tracks and maybe I could find me something there because you can usually find junk anywhere along them tracks, and maybe if I was lucky it would be the right kind of junk.

Me and Courage was walking down the tracks, and about the only thing we was finding was railroad spikes. They was too big to use for nails, so I just let 'em be.

As we walked a little farther I noticed just over the hill was a chair. It was a living room chair with red cloth. It was ripped and torn and some of the stuffing was coming out of it, but I thought I'd be able to use it in The Lodge.

Now, what a chair was doing out here for, I had no idea, but it was here and I was going to use it. So I went down to it to see if I could try and get it up the hill.

As I went down to it, I got a bunch of dirt and rocks in my shoes, and I had to stop and empty them because they was kind of sharp. Then I got tangled up into a bunch of briars that was wrapped around the chair and didn't think I was ever going to get it out of that briar patch – or me, either, for that matter.

It seemed like that any time I moved, the briars would stick into me just as hard as they could, and they hurt, too. But I was going to get that chair out of the briars somehow or other, and I wasn't going to give up even if them briars stuck me to death.

After quite a bit of pulling and bleeding I finally got that chair free from the briars and started pulling it up the hill.

It was a lot heavier than I thought it would be. My fists were all scratched up and I could feel my face bleeding from a scratch, but I kept pulling that chair up the hill.

I got halfway up when I had to stop and rest some. I'm not sure that was a good idea because I lost my momentum, but I simply had to rest. I sat in the squatted position while I tried to work up the strength to pull the chair on up the hill.

I got to wondering if I should try and get below the chair and see if I could push it up the hill instead of pulling it. So I tried to get around the chair to get underneath it so I could start my pushing, but when I moved to the side of the chair it twisted on me and I knew it was going to fall down the hill.

I tried to hold it, but my back started to strain and I had to let go of it, and when I did, it flipped three times down the hill and landed back down in them briars. It looked like it was hung up even worse than it was before.

Now I had to do all of this over again, and I didn't know if I could or not because what little I did already has made me dog tired. That's when Courage came down to where I was and began licking me in the face, which just made me angry. I was in no mood for face licking at that moment.

Then I looked over to my right and seen an old rope lying there. I looked at Courage, though it's not too hard to look at him when he's licking your face, and then I hit upon an idea: I'll take that rope and tie one end to the chair and the other end to Courage and I'll let him pull it up the hill.

So I got the rope and got down into them briars and tied one end to the chair leg, and then I climbed up the hill to where Courage was and looped it around his neck and knotted it, hoping to not strangle the little guy, and I was ready to go.

But Courage wasn't.

That crazy goat wouldn't budge. He just sat there and did nothing. The entire time I've known him, I've never known him not to move. The one time I needed him to run, he wouldn't run. Goats are very frustrating animals.

So I got above him and grabbed ahold of his horns and started pulling on him. He did finally move a little, and then I think he realized what I was trying to do, and he stormed up the hill faster than I had ever seen anything move in my life.

The thing was, when he got to the top he didn't stop. He just kept running. It wouldn't have been so bad if he was running toward the house, but he was running the wrong way, and if he kept running that way he was going to end up in Bristol, and I had no desire to go to Bristol this morning.

"Stop, you stupid goat! You're going the wrong way!" I shouted, but it was like talking to one of my sissies – he wasn't going to do anything that I told him to.

So I gave chase because my chair was falling apart. Pieces were flying everywhere from it and I knew that I wasn't going to have nothing left of that chair when my goat stopped running. And there was no certainty that he was going to stop running either.

I kept shouting and screaming for him to stop, but he didn't. Then the rope broke and that chair rolled down the hill and right into a small pond and sunk to the bottom. I looked on down the track and Courage stopped his running and came back to where I was standing.

What a lousy morning this has turned out to be. All that work to get that chair up here was for nothing.

Courage looked up at me and then jumped on my chest for me to pet him and I did.

People are out in the world helping other people or coming up with new discoveries to help make people well, and here I was with a goat on my chest petting it in the middle of a railroad track.

It was kind of a dumb morning for me.

CHAPTER
FORTY-FIVE

THE NEW BOY

I was working on The Lodge pert near all day when I decided to head down to the house and get me a drink of water.

When I got down there, I seen Suzie and Sally on the front porch looking in the window. They were looking into the piano room, and every couple of seconds they would turn to each other and giggle.

I went up to them and asked them what they was looking at, and they told me to go away. Just told me right up like they was too good to even talk to me.

Well, I wasn't going to put up with that, so I pushed 'em to the side and looked in the window, and there I seen Mary teaching a new boy that I had never seen before.

I turned to my sissies and asked, "Are you two just standing here looking at that fellow in there?"

"We sure are," said Suzie. Sally added, "And we're enjoying ourselves big time."

They then giggled like girls do, and I shook my head like boys do.

"We think he's the cutest thing that's come out of these mountains in some time," said Sally.

Then Suzie tried to trap me right in the middle of the whole thing to where I knew an explosion of some kind was sure enough to follow.

She said, "Why don't you go in there and talk to that boy and ask him which one of us he likes best, and we'll date him on the front porch tonight."

I tell you what the truth is, and you probably know it before I say it, my sissies are crazy.

I said, "Do you two even know what the feller's name is?"

Suzie just stared at me blankly and said, "I don't understand your point."

"Don't you think you ought to know who he is before you get ready to kill him?" I asked.

"We ain't going to kill him, Price," Suzie says. "We're going to date him and we're going to date him until his eyes bulge right out of his head. Right, Sally?"

"I reckon so. Besides, if we were going to kill anyone, it'd be you."

"I'd like to see you try," I said real big like.

"It'd be easy to do," says Sally. "We'd just pretend we was a snake and you'd kill yourself with the hoe."

They both started laughing and I really didn't have a comeback for 'em. I hate it when that happens. I usually can come up with something pretty quick like, but it wasn't happening this time. I sure wished I had a fistful of Mary's mashed potatoes at that very moment. I was also pretty sure that the hoe incident was going to haunt me for some time to come, so I decided to go back to what we was originally talking about and try and save that poor boy at the piano from having to go through a similar situation of not having a comeback when they set in on him.

"Well, if you two like him so much then you should go in there and ask him out on the front porch yourselves."

"We can't do that," said Suzie.

"Why not?" I asked.

"Because we're ladies, you dumb boy," said Suzie.

"When did that start?" I said real loud, which brought the window up and scared the three of us plumb to death.

There standing in the window was Mary, and she didn't look like she was pleased to see the three of us at all.

"What are you three yelling about out here?"

"Nothing," said Suzie.

"Ain't right either," I said. "They's been standing out here watching that boy in there playing the piano and giggling and poking at each other. That's what they've been doing. I seen 'em."

"We're going to poke you if you don't hush," said Suzie.

"And they'll be no giggling either," Sally added, but I wasn't scared.

"You three get on out of here," Mary yelled at us in a whisper. "You'll mess up his concentration."

"What's his name?" asked Sally.

"Don't you mind that any. Now scat!"

Then Mary let down the window and went back over to the piano, and I'm guessing she warned him about the ambush that might be awaiting him when he left.

Though Mary told Sally and Suzie to scat, they didn't. They still stood there looking in the window at that feller.

"He sure is pretty," said Sally.

"Boys ain't pretty," I said.

"They are so," Sally said. Then she said, "Well, some of 'em."

Then they both looked at each other and started laughing. They didn't need to tell me that they were laughing at me neither. So I just set the record straight for 'em.

"Boys ain't pretty. They can be rugged, handsome, or peculiar, but they can't be pretty. It's the way it is, and two girls on the front porch can't change the way it is, so there."

That's when Suzie stuck her tongue out at me. It almost got ugly after that, but I stayed grownup about it.

I said, "And another thing, little Miss Tongue hanging out of her mouth, you can't date no other boys because you're already dating Billy."

"Not anymore," she said.

"I reckon so," I said.

"I reckon not."

"How do you come upon that?" I asked.

"Because I don't have a ring on my finger," she said and held her hand aloft like she was calling a big ol' bird to land on it or something. "And that means I can date whoever I want, and I want to date that boy at the piano."

"You do know that Billy can play the piano just as good as that feller in there can."

"But he don't look as handsome as that boy does. He just looks peculiar," said Sally.

I just knew teaching my sissies a new word would come back to haunt me.

"Well, Billy ain't going to like this one bit."

"I don't care what Billy likes," said Suzie.

"He might have to fight him then," I said, which got both of my sissies thinking, and I'm pretty sure their thinking was heading into a direction I didn't mean for it to go.

"That might be fun," said Suzie.

"What do you mean?" asked Sally.

"The winner could get me and the loser would get you."

"Why am I stuck with the loser?" Sally asked.

"Because I'm older and prettier."

"I'll fix that prettier than me bit up with a fist to the mouth."

That's when that boy came out of the front door and my two sissies took off running around the corner of the house.

That boy stood at the front door as if he was a bit surprised to see me standing there. I just nodded to him.

He said, "Hello."

I said, "Hello."

"I'm John Watkins."

"Are you now?" I replied.

He looked at me like I was accusing him of something, though I wasn't, but I did understand why he might think that.

I said, "How fast can you run, John?"

"I'm pretty fast. Of course, I can run faster when I'm wearing my green pants. Are you wanting to race? If you are, I can run home and get 'em."

I have to admit that his green pants comment kind of threw me. But I regrouped, as they say, and continued on.

"No, I'm not meaning to race you. I'm meaning to save your life."

"I don't understand," said John.

That's when he caught sight of my sissies standing at the corner of the house looking right at him.

I didn't really need to say anything else after that.

He took off running as fast as he could get his legs a-moving, and my sissies took off after him. Poor feller, he might have made it if he had been wearing his green pants.

CHAPTER
FORTY-SIX

THE BIRTHDAY GIFT

You ain't going to believe this!

This truly is the best day of my life, and it happened on my birthday! Why, it is so great that it even passes the day me and Billy found that baseball or I discovered Batman.

I got up this morning just like I always do, not even thinking about it being my birthday. I went toward the kitchen to get me some breakfast and as soon as I walked in, Mommy, Sally, Suzie, and Mary all hollered, "Happy birthday!"

I was shocked. They had the whole kitchen all dressed up with a banner that said "Happy Birthday Price" on it, and they was wearing paper hats made out of old newspapers, and there was a cake setting in the middle of the kitchen table.

I have to say that I couldn't think of anything at all to say. I was just overwhelmed by everything.

They all gave me a hug.

"Are you surprised?" asked Suzie.

"I sure am. I forgot about it being my birthday."

"How do you forget something like that?" asked Sally.

"He's practicing for when he gets older," said Mommy.

"Do you want a piece of cake?" asked Mary.

"I sure do."

So Mary cut me a piece of cake and it tasted good, which was a pretty good indication that Mommy made it.

Then they all wanted me to come into the piano room because they had me a present. I didn't think we had any money for a present, so I got pretty excited. I bet I was even glowing more than Lightning Man could.

I went into the piano room and Mommy and my sissies stayed behind me like they wanted me to be the first to see it. In the middle of the room on the floor was a box wrapped up in newspaper, and on top of it was a smaller box wrapped up in the Sunday comics. So not only did I have one birthday present, I had two!

I was starting to get the jitters or nervous or whatever you call it when your heart beats fast.

"Go ahead and open it," said Mommy.

"Open the big one first," said Suzie.

"He can open first whichever he wants," Mommy said.

So I decided to go ahead and open the little one first, being that it was on top and I had a feeling that the bigger one might be a better present.

I opened it up, being careful not to tear the comics, because not everyone gets to read their wrapping paper later on, and there was a box inside it. I lifted the top and it was paper, brand-new typing paper, clean on both sides so I could do my writing. I was happier than I had ever been in my life.

"Do you like it?" asked Mommy.

Did I like it? What kind of crazy question was that? I just got up and hugged her as hard as I ever hugged anyone in my life.

"You still got one to go," said Sally.

I turned and went over to it and ripped the paper off, being it was just the news of the day and not the comics, so I didn't need to be as careful with it, and what sat before me made me scream.

It was a typewriter.

I started jumping up and down and screaming like I've never done before. They were all laughing at me, but I didn't care. I just lost it. I completely lost all control of my emotions.

I hugged everybody. I even hugged the piano. I couldn't believe this just happened.

Finally Mommy got me to settle down enough to where I could start to think. She took a piece of the typing paper and showed me how to load it into the typewriter, and she then told me to type something.

I had no idea what to type.

"Just type your name," Mommy said.

So I did. Of course, I typed it wrong, which made all my sissies laugh at me and made me a little flustered, but I wasn't going to let it ruin this day.

Mommy told me, "You just have to get used to it, is all. Pretty soon you'll be an old pro at typing."

"Is this why you've been working late?" I asked.

"Never you mind about my working habits," Mommy said. "It only matters that my kids have something in their lives that they want. That's all that matters to me. Now, who wants some more cake?"

We all shouted that we did.

So Mary went in and brought the cake out, and the piece she gave me had a candle lit on top of it, and I blew it out and they all cheered.

Then all of us sat in the piano room at six in the morning eating cake for breakfast.

I will never forget this day for the rest of my life. Never ever never!

CHAPTER
FORTY-SEVEN

SHOWDOWN

I was sitting out on the front porch using my typewriter, you know, just trying to get the hang of it and all. Mommy had gone off to work at the hospital and Mary's piano students had started coming in for their lessons, and I made sure they all got a good look at my typewriter. I told 'em everyone that one day I was going to be a great writer. And famous, to boot!

I don't think any of 'em believed me any, but I believed me, and that's what counts. Why, there was one girl that thought my typewriter was a cash register. Girls sure are dumb.

As I was typing, it didn't take me too long to realize that this was going to take some getting used to. All the letters are scattered about this machine like the wind had got ahold of 'em and blew 'em around, and when I go hunting for one of 'em I have some of the awfullest times there ever was. But I'll keep banging away on this thing to practice. I think I'll still keep my journal by writing it out by hand. That way I can save my typewriter for my important work like on Lighting Man and trying to write a story for Scribner's Magazine.

Everything was going fairly normal for the day. When you're typing the day goes by pretty fast. Then I looked up and seen someone coming up the road toting something.

I didn't know who it was at first, and then I realized it was John. That new boy that makes Suzie and Sally giggle.

He came up on the porch and was carrying a brown bag with something in it.

"Howdy, John."

"Howdy."

"Did you come for your piano lesson today?"

"No," he said. "It's not my turn today. My lesson is for the day after tomorrow."

"That's interesting," I told him.

"What is?"

"That your piano lesson is the day after tomorrow, but you're here today."

"When you put it like that, I guess it is interesting," he told me.

"Have you ever seen a typewriter before?" I asked him.

"Yeah. My mom has one."

"Well, this one is probably better than hers."

That's when he looked at my paper in the typewriter that I've been practicing on and said, "No, I think my mom's is better because hers don't make as many mistakes."

I wasn't a big fan of John at that moment.

"Why'd you come here for?" I asked so he wouldn't insult my beautiful typewriter no more.

"My mom wanted to thank Mary for helping me with the piano playing, so she told me to bring her this bag and give it to her."

"What's in the bag?"

"Onions."

"Well, maybe she won't burn 'em then," I said without thinking. "I'll go in and tell her you're here."

I got up and went inside and ran smack dab into Suzie and Sally standing in the doorway all excited.

"What's John out there for?" asked Suzie.

Before I could even say anything concerning onions, Sally butted in.

"I see a present! Did he bring it for me?"

"It's for me," said Suzie.

"He's not going to waste his time bringing a present to the likes of you," said Sally.

"What's that supposed to mean?"

"I'm prettier."

"You are not! I am."

That's when I tried to set them both straight. "It's not for either one of you. It's for Mary."

They both looked at me like I had donkey ears. They didn't understand why he would bring Mary a present. I guess I should have just told them the truth. That it was a present from John's mother and it wasn't nothing more than onions, but for some reason I didn't tell 'em. I guess I liked playing with 'em just a little. You know how little brothers can be. Plus now they'll know how Billy feels when they play with his emotions all of the time.

"What's she getting a present for? She already has a boyfriend," said Sally.

"Now she can have two," I said. "Why, she might marry both John and Junior, then go down to Bristol and start her own cult."

"You can't have two husbands. Besides, John is too young for Mary," said Sally.

"Well, love can't be restrained by age," I said, and then I went over to Mary where she was teaching one of her students.

"Mary."

"What is it, Price?"

"John is on the porch wanting to talk to you."

"Now?"

"Yeah."

"Why?"

"He's got a present for you from his mother," I said quiet-like so Sally and Suzie couldn't hear me.

"What is it?"

"Onions," I whispered.

She was silent for a bit, and she had a strange look come across her face and then she asked, "Does his mother not like me?"

"No, she likes you just fine."

Mary thought it over and then got up and went outside. John gave her the bag and she hugged him and thanked him and his mother. Now, it so happened that Suzie and Sally was watching Mary out there with John, and when she gave him a hug they both charged out onto the porch full of fire.

"Why are you hugging my boyfriend?" said Sally.

"Mine, too," added Suzie.

"What are you two talking about?" asked Mary.

"You've got a man, Mary. You can't have two, and Mommy wouldn't approve of you starting a cult!" shouted Suzie.

Mary thought they had lost their minds and just thanked John again for the present and went on back inside.

Suzie then went over to John and stared him down right hard and said, "What are you doing giving her my present?"

John was ready to run at this point, and Sally knew it, and that's why she came up behind him to where he had no way out.

"What was the present you gave her?" asked Sally.

"It was onions," John told 'em.

"Onions?" they both said right loud.

"What kind of present is that for a girlfriend?" asked Sally.

"Girlfriend?" asked John. "Do you mean Mary likes me?"

Our problems were getting bigger by the second. It appears that John does indeed like Mary, but Mary don't want anything to do with him being that he's just twelve years old and she already has her a sweetie in Junior. And then that's when the world got even hotter for everybody involved, because up the road came Billy, and he was wearing his dating clothes.

I looked at John and whispered to him, "Why don't you just tell my sissies that them onions was from your mommy and not from you?"

"Because if Mary really likes me I want them to be from me."

"But you already told Mary they was from your mommy," I told him, but my telling him that didn't seem to have any effect on him at all.

That's when Billy stood in front of the porch looking a bit confused, though very sporty.

"Who are you?" Billy asked.

"I'm John. Who are you?"

"I'm Billy. Which one of these girls are you trying to date?"

"I'm going after Mary."

"Hold everything!" I shouted. "Someone has got to have some common sense around here. First off, John, you can't date Mary. She has a man and she's too old for you. Secondly, those onions was from your mommy, not you. Thirdly, Billy, why on earth are you here for?"

"I thought I'd try and date somebody."

"Who are you wanting to date?" I asked.

"Anybody that wants to. I'm not particular."

"What's that present you got there?" asked Sally.

"I ain't saying until someone dates me. Whoever dates me can have it."

"Why can't you tell us now?" asked Suzie.

"Because you might not want to date me then and I'd have to go back home and you'd probably keep the present."

Sally and Suzie went over to the corner of the porch and started whispering. Any time two girls start whispering to one another, problems are on the horizon.

They got done with their whispering and came back over to where we was all standing.

Sally said, "I think that what we'll do is–"

Then Suzie struck out at Billy, knocked him down on the ground and straddled him across his chest. Then her and him started tugging over that present.

"Give it to me, Billy!" shouted Suzie.

"I can't breathe!" shouted Billy as best as he could.

"Let it go and I'll let you breathe!"

"No!"

"I said let go!"

"Not until you say you'll date me!"

"Give it up!"

Then that present ripped and marbles went everywhere.

Suzie got up, and she wasn't happy.

"Marbles? What kind of stupid present is that for your sweetie?" Suzie said.

"I think I'm dead," Billy said as he held his hand on his chest and began rubbing it real soft like.

"What kind of stupid place is this for dating? One guy brings marbles and another brings onions! If I'm going to get a man that can give a girl a decent present, then I'm going to have to move somewhere else!" shouted Suzie.

"If you're going to get a man, you're going to have to stop beating them all up," I said.

Sally came over to Billy and knelt down beside him.

"Are you okay?"

"I'll be fine once the soreness goes away."

"They're not bad-looking marbles," said Sally.

"Do you want 'em?" asked Billy. "You can have 'em if you want."

"Sure, I'll take 'em," said Sally.

"Does this mean you're my sweetie?"

"I'm not sure."

"Well, you can't have 'em unless you're going to be my sweetie."

"But I don't know if I want to be your sweetie until I date all the other fellows around this mountain and see what kind of presents they give me."

"You're playing me, aren't you?"

"It's the rules."

"What rules are you talking about?"

"The book of love rules."

"Well, there must be a chapter in there about fighting because Suzie dern near killed me."

Sally stood up and said, "I'm going to have to do me some thinking. I'll talk to you tomorrow."

Sally and Suzie headed back into the house. John came over to Billy and pulled out a handful of marbles that was in his legendary green pants.

"Do you want to play?" asked John.

"Sure," said Billy.

Then we went off and played us some marbles.

I don't really know who got the best of who today, but I'm sure Sally and Suzie will tell us once they read that rule book of theirs again.

CHAPTER
FORTY-EIGHT

THE HOSPITAL

Well, I had quite a lot happen to me today. Mommy was sick this morning with a real bad stomach ache, and you could tell she was running a fever. I heard her getting up, and I could tell something wasn't right, so I got up and checked on her.

Sure enough, she was sicker than I've ever seen her before. I don't think it was Mary's cooking that did it either, though I can't fully rule it out.

Mary came in the room and seen how sick Mommy was and said for her to get back in bed because she wasn't going anywhere.

"I have to go to work," Mommy said.

"Not like this you won't," said Mary.

"I've got to get my hours in. If I don't get 'em in, they'll not pay me a week's pay. I've got no choice."

"I'll do it," I said.

They both looked at me like I was crazy, but I wanted to do it. Mommy has been working hard, and she bought me that typewriter and all of that paper, so the least I could do was go into work for her when she was sick.

"It's my job as the only man in the house to help out more with paying the bills and such," I said. "I'm twelve years old now, and I have to start pulling my part of the providing around here."

"You don't understand," said Mommy. "This is hard work."

"I can handle hard work. You should have seen me tugging that chair up the hill the other day."

"What chair?" Mommy asked.

"It don't matter what chair, it just matters that I'm not afraid of hard work."

"Do you understand what kind of hospital this is?" asked mommy.

"I'm not afraid of sick people. Just let me do this for you, Mommy. It's my way of thanking you for the typewriter."

"You don't need to thank me–"

"Yes, I do."

Things were silent for a few seconds, then she gave in.

"Okay. I really appreciate this. You need to talk to Mr. Crippen. He's the one in charge, and he'll tell you what needs to be done."

"I'll do it. Now you go on back to bed."

Mommy started coughing pretty bad, and I think she just gave up on trying to talk me out of it and went on back to bed.

"This is a nice thing you're doing for Mommy," said Mary.

"The typewriter was a better gift than my going in to work for her."

"Just be careful," Mary said.

"I will. Don't forget to feed Courage."

"I'll feed him. You just be safe."

"Don't worry about me."

Mr. Ned came by like he always did to pick up Mommy, and he sure was surprised when I walked out of the house toting a sandwich wrapped in newspaper for lunch.

"Where's your mommy?"

"She's sick, so I'm going to fill in for her today."

"Does she need me to take her to the doctor?"

"No. She said she'd be fine in the morning."

"Do you understand what kind of hospital this is?"

There was that question again.

"A hospital is a hospital. I ain't stupid. I know what hospitals are for," I said as if I knew everything and it wouldn't take too long to find out that I don't.

Mr. Ned drove me to the hospital. We didn't talk much. He did ask me what I had in my wrapped-up newspaper, and I told him a sandwich and for some reason he thought that was pretty funny.

I noticed that the closer we got to the hospital the more nervous I got. When we rounded the bend, he took a right turn and we went up this hill. Then we went around a curve and there I saw the spookiest-looking hospital I had ever seen in my life.

It had a tall tower without any lights coming from it. The only lights I saw was in the lower row of windows and I could see shadows inside walking about.

Mr. Ned drove up underneath a roof that led to the doorway and stopped.

"Do you want me to go in with you?"

"No," I said. "I've got to do this by myself."

"Do you know who to talk to?"

"Mr. Crippen."

Mr. Ned got a strange look on his face and told me, "Good luck."

I got out of the vehicle, put my sandwich in my pocket, and walked toward the front door. As I was walking, I heard Mr. Ned leaving and I had to stop and watch him disappear out of sight. I'd never felt so alone in all of my life than I did at this moment.

I then walked on inside and seen this black woman down on her hands and knees scrubbing the floor.

"Excuse me, but do you know where Mr. Crippen is?"

"He's in his office at the far end of the hall on the left."

"Okay, thank you."

"Don't let him scare you."

"I won't."

Now, I've got no idea what I've got myself into. This Mr. Crippen fellow must be some kind of ghost or something. At least, that's the impression I've been getting so far this morning.

I made my way to the end of the hallway where it was very dark. None of the lights shined in here at all. I knocked on the door and then I heard a few footsteps approaching. The door slowly opened and the scariest man I've ever seen in my life was looking down at me.

"Who knocked on my door?" he asked in a manner that said his door was off-limits.

I was waiting for him to say "fe fi fo fum" at that point. He had on round glasses, was bald on top, was kind of skinny, and had large teeth.

"I'm Price Mullins."

"Is that supposed to impress me?"

"No. I was here because my mother couldn't come to work today because she was sick so I–"

"Who are you talking about?"

"Oh, Patricia Mullins. I'm her–"

"If she doesn't work, she doesn't get paid," he said.

"I know that. You see, that's why I'm here. I'm her son, Price Mullins, and I was going to fill in for her today."

"I didn't hire you to do Mrs. Mullins' work. I hired her to do it. If she doesn't do it, then I will not pay her or anyone else for that matter. How dare anyone think they can hire someone in their place to do their work! I do the hiring and I will do the firing. If your mother won't work, then she is fired."

He slammed the door in my face.

I was terrified because I may have just got Mommy fired instead of helping her out like I had planned.

I knocked on the door again, but he didn't come open it, so I just opened it myself and went inside.

"Sir," I said, but got no further than that before he started yelling at me.

"What are you doing coming into my office without permission?!"

I have to admit, I was pretty scared right then, and if this wasn't about my mommy, I would have done and took off running as fast as I could.

I said, "Sir, my mommy needs this job, and I can't let her get fired because I'm here instead of her. She's sick. She didn't mean to be, but she is. That's the only reason she ain't here. Now, all I'm asking is you tell me what to do and I'll do it just like Mommy would. You don't have to pay me anything. All that I ask is that you don't cut any of mommy's pay."

It was quiet for a long time before he just turned away and said, "Go talk to Mrs. Sizemore. She'll tell you what needs to be done."

Then he turned around real quick and came over to where I was and bent down in my face and put his big nose up against mine.

"Don't ever come into my office again like that or I will eat you. Do you understand me, boy?"

"You'll never see me again, I can promise you that."

He went back over to his desk and I got out of there as quick as I could.

I walked back into the front of the hospital and seen the lady that I had seen earlier getting up off of her knees and picking up her bucket of soapy water.

"Did you find him?" she asked.

"Yeah."

"Did he scare you?"

"Yeah."

"Thought he would."

"Does he scare you?"

"He tries, but old black women don't scare anymore."

"He said he'd eat me."

She walked over to me and looked behind my ears.

"Well, if he does he'll be coughing up dirt for some time."

"Do you know Mrs. Sizemore?"

"That's me."

"He told me you'd tell me what to do."

"Who are you?"

I told her who I was and about Mommy and she seemed to be really touched by what I was doing and then told me what to do.

"I need you to go into each of the rooms and empty the trash cans and sweep. The broom is in the closet over there, and you'll also see a large garbage can with wheels on it. When you empty the room's trash, you put 'em in that and then you take it out and put it in the big bin out back. Got it?"

"Yes, ma'am."

"I'm not a ma'am. You can call me Flossy."

"Okay."

Flossy then left and I went to the closet and did what she said for me to do.

The first room I went in, there was an old man asleep who looked like he was dead. The trash can was beside his bed and I was pretty creeped out to walk over there to him to reach down and get it. But I went and I bent down and got the trash can, turned to empty it, turned back around and set the can down as quietly as possible. Then he suddenly grabbed me.

"He's trying to kill me!" the old man shouted. I struggled to get away from him as he had his arm up around my throat with his forearm applying so much pressure that I was having trouble breathing.

That's when Flossy came in and got him off of me. She gave him some sort of shot and he calmed down.

"Are you okay?" she asked.

"I guess. What's wrong with him?"

"Did your mother not tell you?"

"Tell me what?"

"This is a mental hospital. You have to watch yourself at all times. Now you go on and do your job and watch yourself."

"Okay."

Flossy left and I went on about my job, and I didn't have any more problems with the patients, though I do have to admit that I did my job as fast as possible.

After I did all of that, I set out to haul all of the dirty clothes to the laundry area, and then I had to help Flossy diaper some of the people. They weren't babies either. They was old people, and it was disgusting as it could be, so much so that I didn't even eat my sandwich and ended up giving it to Flossy to eat. She seemed to like it.

I had to stay late to help fix the supper for the patients, and after that Mr. Ned came and got me.

I have to tell you that I was pretty well shot and fell asleep in the vehicle on my way home.

Mommy was doing a lot better when I got home, and she thanked me for filling in for her. I told her that I would pray hard for her every night so that she doesn't get sick again so I never have to go back to that place as long as I live.

CHAPTER
FORTY-NINE

LISA

Well, today was a day that I never thought would happen to me. It all began with me trying to get Courage unstuck from under the porch. The crazy thing had got up under there and laid down to sleep, and when he woke up, he got up fast and rammed his horns up through the porch to where they was sticking up through the boards.

So there I was spending my whole morning trying to get him unstuck from the porch boards as best as I could. I was trying to push his head down so the horns could clear the hole they made, and then I could drag him out of there from the way he got up under it. But when I would push down, he would push up, and we got nowhere in a hurry. I finally realized I was going to have to crawl up under there and pull down on his head and then drag him out. Man, if I didn't love him so much or was afraid Mommy might trip over his horns and fall, I'd just leave him under there.

So I got up under there and grabbed his horns and pulled down. He fought me for a bit, but I think he was so tired he just pretty much let me do with him what I pleased. I finally got him free and began dragging him out from under there, and once he seen daylight, he bolted and knocked me right down into a mud puddle that was beside the house.

I was so angry that I thought I was going to make that puddle water boil.

That's when I seen her.

On the porch was a girl in the prettiest blue dress that I had ever seen. She had long blond hair and she was holding her piano book against her chest looking at me like I was the craziest thing she had ever seen in her life.

"What are you doing in the mud puddle?" she asked.

"I was getting my goat free and he knocked me down."

"I don't see no goat."

"He's around."

"Is he a ghost goat?"

"No, he ain't a ghost goat. Do you think I'm making this up?"

She looked all about the yard and then back at me.

"Looks like it."

Then she headed on inside as I sat there in that mud puddle and began thinking about what just happened.

I knew at that moment that I was in love. And wet.

I got up and went upon the porch to look through the window to watch her. I couldn't take my eyes off of her because she was so pretty.

Unfortunately when a boy is standing on the front porch watching the girl he is fixing to marry play the piano while covered in mud, he tends to forget that he has two other sissies about to make his life miserable.

"What are you looking at in there?" asked Sally.

Her voice just about made me start scrambling up the side of the house. I didn't know she was anywhere around and I had done thought I was being attacked by a monster. And I wasn't too far off, either.

So I tried to keep in control of the situation as best as a boy can while facing his two sissies.

"Nothing. I'm going fishing."

That's when Suzie looked in the window and started laughing.

"Looks like Price has a sweetie."

Sally looked in and seen that girl playing the piano, and she started laughing and then they started singing, "Price has a sweetie! Price has a sweetie!"

"I do not!"

Now, I don't know what I said that for. I did think she was the cutest thing and I wouldn't mind being her sweetie at all, but when your sissies are taunting you, a boy goes on defense in a hurry.

"Then why was you looking in that window for if you're not sweet on Lisa?" asked Suzie.

"I wasn't. Hey, how do you know her name?"

"She's our friend," said Sally. "Mommy has done some sewing for her family, and we would all hang out together and talk about boys."

"What did she say about boys?" I asked.

"Why do you care?" asked Suzie.

"I was just making conversation," I told 'em. Boy, I need to work on my sissy defenses big time.

"Well, you can forget about dating her because she has too high of standards for you to ever meet," said Suzie.

"Like what?"

"For one thing, she don't want no man with mud all over his clothes, and she wants a man with little ears," said Sally.

"I don't care."

"Sure you don't," said Sally. "You better not let Billy see her or he'll be bringing a present to her by sunset."

"Don't you all tell Billy about Lisa!"

I said that before thinking, and it pretty much gave away the fact that I had done and found the woman I was going to marry.

Sally and Suzie started laughing and then they left while singing, "Price is in love!"

When they left, I turned and looked in the window some more at Lisa. Until Mary rapped on the window and told me to go up in the woods or something and stop bothering her students.

So I headed on out to do me some fishing and decided if I had woman problems I needed to talk to an expert. And the only expert I knew of was Billy.

CHAPTER
FIFTY

GOODBYE MRS. COLLINS

I was sitting out on the front porch resting. Courage had got his head hung up in the tire swing earlier, and it took the whole family about half an hour to get him out of the thing.

As I was sitting there, Billy came by and I got ready to tell him all about Lisa and ask him how I could get her to like me real good. But before I was able to ask, he told me something that completely shocked me.

"Did you hear about Mrs. Collins?"

"No. What about her?" I asked.

"She died."

I couldn't believe my ears. "She died?"

"Yeah. She died last week and they buried her the day before yesterday."

"Are you sure?"

"I'm sure."

We both just sat there and didn't say much.

"It's strange, ain't it?" I said. "I mean I didn't know teachers died."

"Teachers die, too," Billy said.

"Well, I know that they die, but I thought they died after they was finished teaching, not while they was still doing it."

"Are you going to be okay?"

"I don't know," I said. "Mrs. Collins was always nice to me. In fact, I think she was my favorite teacher of all."

"Do you want to go to her grave?"

"I think I should."

So me and Billy headed toward the graveyard to say our goodbyes.

We got there and I stood at the grave. It had a tombstone on it that said *Martha Collins 1881-1941*. When I read those words, I could feel a tear run down my face.

"You going to be okay, Price?" Billy asked me.

"Yeah. I'll be back later."

I went home and got my journal that I've been writing and put it in that bread box I had found and brought it back to the grave, and here I am now writing this part down.

I got to thinking about Mrs. Collins and all she did for me and the fact that I never thanked her for not only teaching me, but by telling me that I should be a writer. If she didn't tell me that, I wouldn't have written any of this down. So I've decided to give her my journal.

Now, I know that she can't read it, but I think she would understand why I left it for her. I just had to do something to thank her for all she's done, and I thought this was the best thing I could do.

Here's my journal, Mrs. Collins. I thank you for being my teacher and I'll always love you.

Your student, Price Mullins.

ABOUT THE AUTHOR

Kyle Owens lives in the Appalachian Highlands and his stories have appeared in Liguorian, Eastern Iowa Review, and Ahoy Comics, among others. His romantic comedy novel, A Mountain Christmas Wedding, was published by Books to Go Now. His cartoon collection, "The New Yorker Hates My Cartoons," was published by Clash Books.

Be sure to also check out Kyle's new, The Vegas Chantly Mysteries, published by OffBeatReads.

Connect with Kyle:
Amazon page: https://www.amazon.com/stores/Kyle-Owens/author/B07YLCCHKZ
X: @KyleOwe02309720

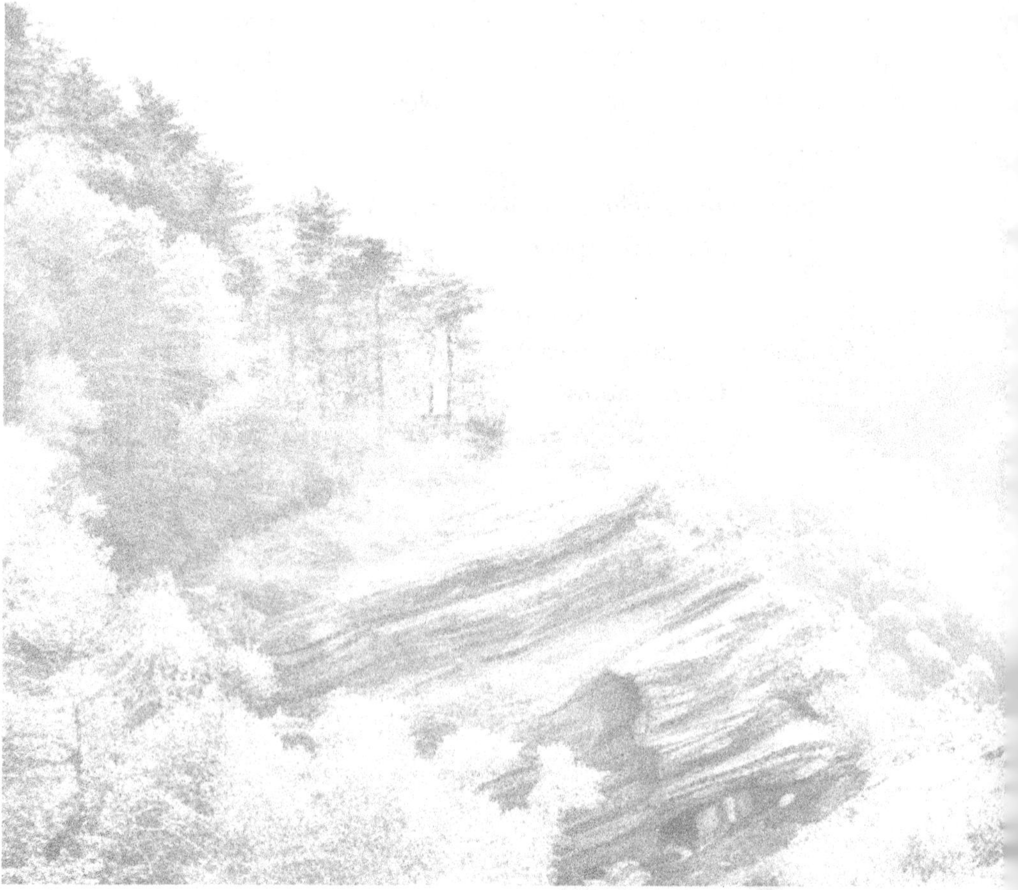

Printed in the USA
CPSIA information can be obtained
at www.ICGtesting.com
LVHW091156151123
763986LV00070B/1946

9 781950 464524